12.20

D0968617

Warren raced on.

Partway down the second ridge, he looked at his watch again. Eight thirty-one. Maybe he had remembered the time wrong. Maybe the mountain didn't erupt at eight-thirty.

He stopped running and took a deep breath. He stuck his right foot out in front of him and straightened the leg and hung his head toward his knee, stretching out his tired leg muscles. He held the pose for a few seconds and then did the same thing with his left leg. While he stretched, he watched the mountain warily.

Just as he straightened up, the ground dropped from beneath his feet and he fell backward onto the gravel road. A low rumbling noise, like a faraway freight train coming through the forest, filled the air. Warren scrambled to his feet and looked back.

Too awestruck to run, Warren stared as gigantic slabs moved down the side of the volcano. The volcano was erupting sideways, just as Betsy's article had said . . .

Only this time he was standing in the middle of it all . . . .

Books by Peg Kehret

Cages
Danger at the Fair
Deadly Stranger
Horror at the Haunted House
Night of Fear
Nightmare Mountain
Sisters, Long Ago
The Richest Kids in Town
Terror at the Zoo
FRIGHTMARES™: Cat Burglar on the Prowl
FRIGHTMARES™: Bone Breath and the Vandals
FRIGHTMARES™: Don't Go Near Mrs. Tallie
FRIGHTMARES™: Desert Danger
FRIGHTMARES™: The Ghost Followed Us Home
FRIGHTMARES™: Race to Disaster
FRIGHTMARES™: Screaming Eagles
FRIGHTMARES™: Backstage Fright
The Blizzard Disaster
The Flood Disaster
The Volcano Disaster

THE VOLCANO DISASTER

PEG KEHRET

Aladdin Paperbacks
New York   London   Toronto   Sydney   Singapore

This book is a work of fiction. Any references to historical events, real people, or real locales are used fictitiously. Other names, characters, places, and incidents are the product of the author's imagination and any resemblance to actual events or locales or persons, living or dead, is entirely coincidental.   .

First Aladdin Paperbacks edition August 2002
First Minstrel Books paperback edition October 1998

ALADDIN PAPERBACKS
An imprint of Simon & Schuster
Children's Publishing Division
1230 Avenue of the Americas
New York, NY 10020

Printed in the United States of America
10 9

ISBN 0-671-00968-0

*For Pat MacDonald,
with appreciation for her talent
and her enthusiasm*

ACKNOWLEDGMENTS

My thanks to Marilyn Kamcheff, friend and fellow writer, for sharing with me her extensive collection of Mount Saint Helens literature, including special-edition newspapers from the week of the eruption.

Thanks, also, to Michelle O'Donnell, Lead Interpreter at the Mount Saint Helens Visitor Center near Castle Rock, Washington, who read my manuscript and suggested ways to improve it.

CHAPTER

1

Warren Spalding felt split in two. One half of him wanted to hurry into Gram's house and tell her he was glad to see her. The other half refused to get out of the car.

That second half wanted to kick and yell like an angry two-year-old, and say how much he resented having to live with Gram for six months. Not that he didn't love Gram; he did. But there had already been too many changes in Warren's life. He didn't want another one.

"It will be better for you," Mom had said. "With me going to college and working, too, I'll never be home. This way you and

Gram can talk to each other. She's excited about having someone to cook for again, and you don't have to change schools; you'll still see your friends."

Mom's version of why he was going to live with Gram was not the whole story. The real reason, and Warren knew this even though it had never been spoken out loud, was that Mom and Gram hoped the change of scene would also change Warren's attitude, and turn him back into the cheerful boy he had been last summer, before his father died.

"Don't count on this move to make me happy," Warren mumbled as Mom stopped the car. Then he saw the hurt look that flashed across Mom's face, and he regretted his words.

It wasn't Mom's fault that he was miserable. The truth is, she was miserable, too, but she was much better at covering up her feelings than Warren was. That is, she covered them up in the daytime, with other people.

Sometimes at night Warren heard her crying in bed, long after she thought he was asleep. Once, he had stood outside her door, debating whether or not to knock and offer to make some popcorn or hot chocolate, and he heard Mom throw something, throw it hard at the wall. He heard the *thwack* as it hit, and then he heard her say, "I can't do this alone, Dan. It's too hard. I need you here."

It made Warren's skin crawl to hear her talk to Dad that way, as if Dad were still alive and sitting beside her. As if Dad had chosen to get broadsided by a drunk driver.

Warren had crept back to the solitude of his own bed and never listened at Mom's door again.

Gradually Mom cried less and smiled more, and now, six months after the accident, she acted really excited about going back to college for the winter and spring quarters, and finishing the degree in biology that she'd always wanted.

Warren knew she worried about him. He even felt guilty for making her worry, but he couldn't change how he felt. It was as if a glass wall now separated him from the rest of the world. He ate, went to school, and talked to his friends, but he did it all without enthusiasm. He no longer *cared.* His grades had slipped so much that Mom had gone for a conference with Mr. Munson, Warren's sixth-grade homeroom teacher. Since then, Warren had forced himself to do his homework, but he did the minimum required.

"Warren! You're here!" Gram's excited voice welcomed him, and the unhappy half of Warren slid out of sight as he got out of the car and went to hug her.

"You get Danny's old room," Gram said. "It's hard for me to climb the stairs now, so I never go up there. It's a mess—still full of Grandpa's projects—but I thought you'd like having the upstairs all to yourself."

Warren carried his suitcase up to the room that had been his father's when Dad was Warren's age. It no longer looked like a young boy's bedroom, because after Warren's dad grew up, Grandpa had taken over that room for his inventions. The large desk and wooden table were piled with notes, drawings, and working models of Grandpa's many gadgets.

When Warren was little, he had loved watching Grandpa tinker with his inventions. Grandpa used to explain how everything worked, and even though Warren only understood about half of it, he liked listening. Grandpa always let him take something apart—an old alarm clock or a nonworking radio—and then, on Warren's next visit, they would put it back together again.

Now Warren was good at figuring out how things work. Just last week he had fixed Mom's toaster after the Small Appliance Repair Service had told her to buy a new toaster because the old one was beyond help.

"You are just like your grandpa," Mom had said.

Grandpa had held the patents on three devices—one to heat steering wheels so drivers never need gloves, one to suck the seeds and juice out of cantaloupe and other small melons before they are cut, and one that holds both ends of a jump rope and turns it automatically so that the person jumping does not have to hang on to the rope.

Of the three patented inventions, only the Seed Sucker ever got manufactured commercially, and it had not sold well. Grandpa's biggest technical success was the cellular telephone. Unfortunately, he invented it after someone else had taken out the patent on the technology, so Grandpa's achievement came too late.

The rest of Grandpa's ideas had never gone beyond his workroom. Grandpa had thought he had the solution to lots of problems, but none of his inventions had worked out the way he expected.

Just like me, Warren thought. My life isn't turning out the way I expected, either. This was the year that he and Dad had planned to go camping in the mountains over Thanksgiving vacation. And this was the year that Dad was going to be the assistant coach for Warren's basketball team.

Instead, Warren and Mom and Gram ate Thanksgiving dinner together at Gram's house, and tried to think of reasons to be thankful. And Warren decided not to go out for basketball.

Warren set his suitcase on the bed. More than three years had passed since Warren had been in that room; after Grandpa died, there had been no reason to go up there.

He looked at some of the diagrams that littered the tabletop, surprised by how detailed and professional they were—like an architect's blueprints for a house. It might be interesting to study Grandpa's plans and drawings. He picked up a notebook and began to read.

As he read Grandpa's notes and studied the diagrams, Warren's curiosity awoke. Before Grandpa died, he had been working on an Instant Commuter. According to Grandpa's notes, the Instant Commuter would stop air pollution, save the environment, and revolutionize the way people travel.

The device looked simple. An oblong box, the size of a shoe box, fit into a backpack so it could easily be carried. A slim cord ran from the box to a pencil-like pointer that Grandpa called the probe.

According to the plans, the person wearing the Instant Commuter would turn it on, touch the pointed end of the probe to a map, and in less than a minute the Instant Commuter would transport the person to that place.

There would be no travel time, no looking at the scenery as you move through the streets, no flying through the air like Peter Pan. You could be in Chicago one minute and then, less than sixty seconds later, you could be in San Diego. Or Florida. Or London.

When the probe was not in use, it slipped

into a special pocket on the side of the backpack, ready for the traveler's trip home.

"This is my masterpiece," Grandpa had written in his Instant Commuter notebook. "I am creating a solution to one of Earth's greatest problems."

I should try to test this invention, Warren thought. If it worked the way Grandpa said it would, it really would change the way people travel.

For the first time since Dad's accident, Warren felt a glimmer of excitement. Maybe I can get the Instant Commuter to work, he thought. Maybe I can follow the directions and do what Grandpa had planned to do.

Maybe *I* will solve the problem of air pollution.

CHAPTER

2

Warren gaped at his teacher as if Mr. Munson had just grown an extra head. *Twenty pages?* Mr. Munson expected the written reports to be twenty pages long?

Warren's friend, Skipper, rolled his eyes and whispered, "Call the medics. The man has lost his mind."

Mr. Munson ignored the groans and protests of the class. "Since you will be working with a partner," he said, "that is only ten pages each—not an unreasonable amount." He peered over the top of his glasses at the students. "I assume you chose 'Natural Disasters' from the list of elective classes because you have some interest in the subject. Once you begin, I think you'll find your work fascinating."

Skipper nudged Warren with his elbow and scribbled "Let's be partners" on the back of his notebook.

Warren nodded. If he had to write twenty whole pages about a disaster, he might as well do it with Skipper, who knew the batting average of every Major League baseball player, past and present, and who had the amazing ability to wiggle his left ear and raise his right eyebrow up and down at the same time.

"I have assigned partners and topics for this project," Mr. Munson said. Amidst another chorus of groans and complaints, he handed each student a paper that listed the name of his or her partner, the due date, and which disaster they were supposed to study for the twenty-page report.

Warren quickly scanned his paper, hoping that Mr. Munson had paired him with Skipper. Instead, he saw "Warren Spalding/ Betsy Tyler."

Oh, great. Twenty pages, and Betsy for a partner. Mr. Munson should let them choose their own partners instead of assigning them. Warren would never have chosen Betsy, that's for sure.

Betsy was a walking trivia quiz. She had what Mr. Munson politely called an insatiable curiosity and quirky memory, which meant Betsy was snoopy, read constantly, and remembered odd facts. She often spouted peculiar bits of information on strange subjects.

Just yesterday, when Mr. Munson announced that class pictures would be taken next week, everyone else had started talking about what they would wear for the pictures. Not Betsy. Betsy had said, "The basic concept of photography was established in 1727 by Johann Schulze, a German who discovered that silver turns dark when it's exposed to light."

Everyone quit talking about clothes and stared at Betsy.

"How do you happen to know that, Betsy?" Mr. Munson asked.

"I read about photography in an encyclopedia," Betsy explained. "And I remembered that part because my grandparents' last name is Schulze." She smiled. "Same spelling."

Betsy's weird facts and unexpected

quotes weren't the worst part of having her for a partner, though. Warren could put up with Betsy's instant recall of unimportant facts, and it might even be an asset for a twenty-page report. What really bothered him was the fact that Betsy was a girl, with sparkling eyes and deep dimples and hair the color of caramel corn.

Lately, girls made Warren feel awkward. Whenever he talked to a girl, especially a cute and nice one, like Betsy, he had the odd feeling that his hands and feet were growing larger right on the spot, or that he had dandruff, or that bits of lettuce from his lunch were lurking between his front teeth.

Writing a twenty-page report would have been bad enough with Skipper. He could not imagine spending that much time with Betsy.

He glanced at Betsy. She didn't look thrilled about the partnership, either, but she shrugged her shoulders at him as if to say, "There isn't much we can do about it."

At least, he thought, Mr. Munson gave us an exciting topic. He read the assignment again: "The Eruption of Mount Saint Helens; May 18, 1980." Warren didn't know anything about volcanoes, except that they were mountains that blow their tops. He did know that Mount Saint Helens was in Washington State. Warren lived in Washington, so the research would be especially interesting.

Betsy walked to his desk and stood beside him. "Do you want to go to the library together so we can each take half the material to read?" she asked.

"Okay," Warren said. Brilliant answer, he told himself as he stood up. That should impress her.

On the way to the library Betsy said, "I saw you in my neighborhood yesterday."

"You did?" Warren rubbed his tongue across his front teeth, relieved when it failed to dislodge any chunks of lettuce.

"Yes. At that white house on Shepherd Road, the one with the picket fence."

"My grandma lives there," Warren said. "I'm staying with her for a while."

Betsy's whole face lit up with a smile. "How lucky! I live at the other end of that block. It will be easy for us to get together to work on our report."

Me and my big mouth, Warren thought. The last thing he needed was for Betsy to come to Gram's house and find out about Grandpa's inventions. With her curiosity, she might get interested and try to help him, and Warren wanted to complete the inventions by himself. Especially the Instant Commuter.

After arriving at Gram's house last Sunday, he had spent the rest of the day studying Grandpa's drawings and models. He did not tell Gram or Mom what he was doing. He knew they assumed he was lying on the bed, staring at nothing and feeling sorry for himself, the way he had spent much of his free time for the last six months.

Instead, Warren had read and reread Grandpa's information about the Instant Commuter. He examined the invention, inside and out, and memorized Grandpa's instructions for how to use it.

By the time Mom called upstairs to tell him she was leaving, Warren was so absorbed that he didn't hear her and she had to call again. Reluctantly Warren had left the Instant Commuter and gone downstairs to say goodbye.

"Try to act pleasant," Mom had whispered, "for Gram's sake."

"Have fun in college," Warren responded.

"And don't worry about me. I plan to pig out on Gram's apple pie."

Mom had smiled then, clearly relieved.

"If he's expecting apple pie, I'd best get into the kitchen," Gram said, and she bustled off.

As soon as Mom left, Warren hurried back upstairs to his secret project. Right from the start he knew he wouldn't tell anyone what he was trying to do. Not even Gram.

Since Sunday he had spent every spare second studying the Instant Commuter.

Betsy spoke again. "We could work together on Saturdays."

Warren blinked, realizing Betsy had been talking to him all along, while he was thinking about the Instant Commuter. Now she looked at him expectantly, waiting for him to respond.

"I'm, uh, I'm already doing a project on Saturdays," he said. "I might not be able to work on our volcano report except at school."

"There won't be enough time during school to do it right," Betsy said. "But if Saturdays don't work for you, we can stay after school, or maybe meet in the evenings or on Sunday afternoon. You can come to my house, if you like, or we could go to the public library."

Warren nodded, relieved that they had reached the school library and were now expected to be quiet.

As they entered the library, Betsy whispered, "Before printing was invented, books were so valuable that they were sometimes chained to the shelves to keep people from stealing them."

Warren tried to imagine heavy chains connecting the spines of the books to the library shelves. It was unthinkable.

They found one book on Mount Saint Helens and two general books on volcanoes that included a chapter about Saint Helens. Warren checked out the first book and Betsy took the other two. They agreed to read the material as quickly as possible and then trade.

On the way back to Mr. Munson's classroom, Warren tripped on the bare hallway and nearly fell. He regained his balance just before he went down.

Betsy ignored his stumble. She said, "I walk my dog past your grandma's house every day. Maybe I'll see you after school."

"Maybe," Warren said. Another clever reply, he told himself. Talking to Betsy makes my feet feel enormous and my brain shut down. How am I going to write a twenty-page report with her?

Besides, Warren didn't really want to think about a volcano right then. He wanted to think about Grandpa's invention. Every time he tinkered with it, his excitement soared. He understood how it was supposed to operate, and he was eager to try it.

It might work, Warren thought. The Instant Commuter really might work!

CHAPTER

3

Saturday, at last.

All week Warren had looked forward to actually running the Instant Commuter. Now he was ready.

He got up at seven, dressed quickly, and spread out Grandpa's Instant Commuter instructions. The last page was a checklist of things to do just prior to turning on the machine.

Carefully he went down Grandpa's checklist, following each command. He made sure the battery was charged. He compared the wiring to the wiring diagrams.

He picked up the probe, unscrewed the blunt end, and pulled the inner workings out of the case. He made sure the ends of the copper wires were tightly twisted together.

Just then Gram's voice broke his concentration. "Warren! Come and have some breakfast."

Since Gram never came upstairs, Warren always left the door open, so he could hear her if she called him.

Warren looked at the clock, surprised that it was already past nine. When he was concentrating on an interesting project, time seemed to disappear.

As he drank a glass of orange juice, Gram lifted a crisp golden waffle out of her waffle iron and plopped it on Warren's plate.

"There are advantages to living with you," he said as he drizzled hot maple syrup over the waffle. "Mom thinks waffles come from the freezer section of the supermarket."

"You're on your own for lunch," Gram said. "My Book Discussion Group is meeting here for salad and dessert. We read a children's book with a local setting, and we're going on a field trip to visit it."

Three waffles later Warren helped with the dishes and then hurried back upstairs.

He put the probe back together. Then he carefully went over all of Grandpa's Instant Commuter drawings again. He reread the notebook. He checked every part of the actual machine.

When he was satisfied that he had everything exactly as it should be, he picked up the Instant Commuter and put it inside the special canvas backpack. He threaded the probe out the small slit in the bottom of the backpack and pulled the cord through.

He slipped his arms through the backpack's straps and settled the backpack on his back. An extra strip of canvas went across his chest between the shoulder straps, as a precaution against losing the Instant Commuter; Warren buckled it securely.

He pulled the probe through a loop on his belt, so the cord that connected it to the rest of the machine hung straight down his side where it couldn't get tangled on something.

He stuck the pointed end of the probe in the pocket of his jeans.

He walked to the mirror over the dresser and gazed at himself. Good. He looked like an average twelve-year-old kid: on the skinny side, with brown hair and a lopsided smile, dressed in faded jeans and a red T-shirt, with an ordinary-looking tan backpack on his back.

If anyone saw Warren, there would be nothing to call attention to the fact that he was using an incredible device that was about to revolutionize the way people traveled.

He opened the map of King County and drew a circle around the location of Pine Lake Middle School. If the Instant Commuter worked—and the hair on Warren's neck prickled just thinking of that possibility—then, when he turned the machine on and touched the tip of the probe to the circle on the map, he would no longer be sitting in this room. Instead, in one minute or less he would be standing in front of his school.

That is, he hoped he would be standing in front of the school, on one of the grassy areas or a sidewalk. What if he ended up on the roof? Or in the middle of 228th Street, with traffic whizzing past? Or, worst of all, inside the school, in the girls' bathroom?

Well, it was Saturday. No one would be

at the school on Saturday. If he landed inside, he wouldn't be seen.

He double-checked his shirt pocket, where he had put the map that showed the location of Gram's house.

One whole page of Grandpa's notebook said:

WARNING!
Before using the Instant Commuter,
be sure you have a map with you that
shows the location where you are now.
Without it, the Instant Commuter can't
take you back home.

As soon as he read that, Warren had photocopied the section of the map that showed Gram's street and put clear tape on it to protect it in case it ever got wet.

The first thing he had done that morning when he started work on the Instant Commuter was put the map of home in his pocket. If he traveled with the Instant Commuter, he wanted to make it a round trip.

Of course, he could easily walk from the school to Gram's house, if he had to, but Gram would wonder why Warren was coming in the door when he had never gone out. Warren didn't want to have to explain.

Besides, Pine Lake Middle School was just his trial run. If that trip went as planned, Warren planned to go farther the next time. Maybe he would go to a University of Washington basketball game in Seattle. Or even a Sonics game. Maybe he would go to Disney World.

He felt the map through the fabric of his shirt. Wherever he went, he would be able to come home any time he chose.

I'm ready, Warren thought.

He slid the probe out of his pocket.

He took a deep breath.

He reached over his right shoulder, stuck his finger in the backpack, and found the On switch at the top of the Instant Commuter.

Click.

Nothing buzzed or hummed or beeped. No lights flashed.

Good, Warren thought. Grandpa had designed the Instant Commuter to be noiseless. If it whirred or rumbled or clanged, and thousands of people used the devices to travel every day, the racket would be terrible.

According to the notebook, Warren "might feel a slight breeze during the transition." There were supposed to be no other physical sensations. So far, so good.

As Warren aimed the pointed end of the probe at the Pine Lake Middle School circle on the map, his hand trembled slightly from excitement.

He paused and took another deep breath. Shaky hands would not be a good thing for this experiment. If he missed the circle by half an inch, he could end up swimming with the ducks in Pine Lake.

He stared at the map and willed himself to be calm. He put his left hand under his right wrist, to steady it. He bent closer to the map, staring at the circle.

His mind raced. Was there anything he had forgotten? Did he remember all of Grandpa's instructions?

He wondered if the Wright brothers were this nervous at Kitty Hawk, before they flew the first airplane.

He decided to count down, the way NASA does when they launch a space shuttle.

Ten . . .

Nine . . .

Eight . . .
Seven . . .
Six . . .
Five . . .
Four . . .
Three . . .
Two . . .

"Hi, Warren! How's it going?"

Warren jerked his hand away from the map. He whirled around to see who had spoken.

Betsy stood behind him, looking curiously at the diagrams of the Instant Commuter.

CHAPTER

"**W**hat are you doing here?" Warren said.

He held the probe behind his back so Betsy wouldn't see it, and he moved toward the center of the table, trying to shield the drawings from Betsy's curious gaze.

He glared at Betsy.

In one hand Betsy held a magazine and a videotape; in the other hand she had a leash. On the end of the leash was the fattest dog Warren had ever seen.

"I'm sorry if I startled you," Betsy said. "I went to the Issaquah Library last night and found this great article about Mount Saint Helens. I brought it over so you can read it. And I checked out a video about Mount Saint Helens that shows what's happened there in the years since the eruption. I thought maybe we could watch it together."

"Oh," Warren said.

"Your grandma told me to come upstairs because she has company."

"Oh."

"Did you read your library book yet?" Betsy asked.

"Not all of it." He had read only the first paragraph before putting it aside to work on the Instant Commuter.

"This article is even better than the library books I got at school," Betsy said. "Did you know that the top of the volcano is one thousand three hundred and thirteen feet lower now than it was before the eruption?"

"No," Warren said. "I didn't know that."

"Well, it is. And not only that, the blast shot out sideways, as well as straight up."

"No kidding."

"That hardly ever happens."

Warren noticed that as Betsy talked, she kept trying to look around him, at the diagrams. He tried to think of something to say that would prevent her from asking any questions about what he was doing.

"Your dog needs to go on a diet," he said.

"This is Creampuff. She *is* on a diet."

"I don't think it's working," Warren said.

At the sound of her name, Creampuff wagged her tail happily.

"She isn't my dog," Betsy continued. "I'm a foster parent for the Purebred Dog Rescue. Creampuff is a purebred Welsh corgi. Her owner moved to England and Creampuff couldn't go because dogs going into England have to be quarantined for six months. Rather than have her caged for so long, her owner decided to give her up. I'm taking care of Creampuff until the Purebred Dog Rescue can find her a permanent home."

Creampuff sniffed Warren's ankle. Warren started to reach down with his free hand, to pet the short brown-and-white dog, but he realized that if he bent over, Betsy would see the drawings. And she would see the cord coming out of the backpack and start asking questions.

He straightened up and kept his hands behind him. "Hi, Creampuff," he said.

"Usually, I only have the dogs for a week

or two," Betsy said. "Creampuff has already been with me for a month. So far no one is interested in adopting her permanently because she's so heavy. When potential adopters see her, they worry that she will have back or leg problems because of the excess weight."

"Why don't you try diet dog food?"

"I started feeding her diet dog food as soon as I got her," Betsy said, "and we do a daily Doggie Weight Loss Walk. We walk two miles every day. So far, Creampuff has lost half a pound."

"It must have come off her tail," Warren said. "The rest of her looks like a stuffed sausage."

"I know. But she's a sweet dog, and it isn't her fault that her previous owner fed her too much. The vet said to try exercise and diet dog food for two months. If they don't work, the next step is *less* dog food, and Creampuff doesn't want that, do you, Creampuff?"

Creampuff gazed lovingly at Betsy and wagged her tail so hard she nearly fell over.

Warren laughed.

"She responds to my tone of voice, rather than my words," Betsy said. "I could tell her she's a horrible ugly dog, but if I said it the right way, she'd be happy."

Creampuff licked Betsy's ankle.

"As soon as Creampuff trims down, lots of people will want to adopt her," Betsy said.

"Take pictures," Warren suggested. "She can be a Before and After ad for diet dog food."

Betsy laid the video on the table, next to the Instant Commuter drawings. She opened her magazine to the page where she had inserted a bookmark, then laid the magazine next to the video.

"Here's the article I found," she said. "It has great pictures, starting with some taken right before Mount Saint Helens erupted. They show the entire blast."

"I'll—um, I'll read the article later," Warren said. "I'm kind of busy right now."

He stared at Betsy, hoping she would take the hint and leave. Instead she said, "How does it work?"

"What?"

She pointed at the top diagram, which was clearly labeled. "The Instant Commuter. How does it work? Is it some kind of model car? You said you had a project, but I didn't think it would be anything so elaborate. Is that what you have in your backpack?"

Warren knew he might as well explain everything. With her curiosity, Betsy would never be satisfied until he did.

But he wasn't quite ready to share his secret. All she had seen was one diagram; she hadn't read the notebook or any of Grandpa's explanations. She didn't know that the Instant Commuter would revolutionize the way people travel and save the world from air pollution.

"It isn't finished," Warren said. "I don't know yet if it will work or not."

"It looks complicated," Betsy said. "Are these drawings of the inside?" She reached for the stack of Instant Commuter diagrams.

Warren's hand shot out to prevent Betsy from picking up the drawings. He still held the probe.

When his hand moved toward the table, to push Betsy's hand away from the drawings, the tip of the probe touched Betsy's magazine.

Instantly Warren felt a gentle vibration between his shoulder blades, where the Instant Commuter hung. He froze, staring in disbelief at what he had done. The moment lasted only a fraction of a second, but during that brief time Warren realized he had never turned off the Instant Commuter.

The probe had not touched a map, but it had touched the magazine picture, and the machine felt different now, as if it were alive.

What if . . . ?

No, Warren thought. It couldn't possibly work on a photograph.

Could it?

He reached his left hand over his right shoulder. The machine felt warm. It was definitely running.

He pushed the switch to Off.

"Is something wrong?" Betsy said.

The vibration continued.

Even after he turned the Instant Commuter off, it was still operating. Once the process began, it must continue until it was finished, regardless of whether the switch was On or Off.

Warren realized he was about to take a trip.

I can't go now, Warren thought. Not in front of Betsy. And not to Mount Saint Helens! That's too far for the first trip. What if something goes wrong?

Warren felt a strong wind blow through his bedroom. Although the papers on the table did not stir, Warren had to close his eyes against the wind.

He dropped the probe, letting it dangle by his side.

He fumbled with the buckle on the strap across his chest. He had to get the machine off. Fast!

He got the buckle undone and slipped the left strap off his shoulder. The Instant Commuter hung at an angle behind his right shoulder.

The wind blew harder; Warren could barely stand up.

"What's the matter?" Betsy said. "You're as white as a snowball."

Warren reached for the second strap.

He felt Betsy's hands grip his shoulders. "What is it?" she said. "Are you sick?"

"Help me get it off!" Warren cried.

"Woof!" barked Creampuff.

Warren pushed frantically on the remaining strap.

The wind blew harder and harder. "Slight breeze," Grandpa had said. It was more like a hurricane. Warren felt as if it would blow him over onto the floor, and he leaned against the edge of the table to keep his balance.

He felt Betsy's hands push the second strap off his shoulder, but the cord to the probe was still inside the loop of Warren's belt. The backpack now hung from the cord.

Warren let go of the table and yanked on the cord, tearing it from the machine.

The Instant Commuter crashed to the floor. Warren flung the probe after it.

"Woof!" yipped Creampuff. "Woof! Woof! Woof!"

"Please be quiet up there," called Gram. "My guests have arrived."

The wind stopped as suddenly as it had begun. It had blown for only twenty seconds, although it had seemed far longer to Warren.

Warren opened his eyes. He was no longer in his bedroom in the upstairs of Gram's house.

He stood on a narrow gravel road that he did not recognize. On both sides of the road, tall fir trees stretched their tips toward the blue sky. Birds chittered in the otherwise silent forest.

The sun was low, as if it were early morning or late afternoon, rather than the middle of the day. Odd, Warren thought. He looked at his watch. It said 11:45.

Far down the road, beyond the trees, a mountain loomed overhead. The peak had the unmistakable indentation of a volcanic crater.

He wished he had a pair of binoculars.

Even without them, he knew. It's the mountain in Betsy's magazine picture, Warren thought.

I am standing at the base of Mount Saint Helens.

CHAPTER

5

Vicky Huron watched out the car window for a glimpse of Mount Saint Helens. She hoped some steam or ash would puff out of the crater today.

Vicky knew that in the last two months, since the volcano had rumbled to life after one hundred and twenty-three years of dormancy, Saint Helens had shot smoke, steam, volcanic ash, and sulfur gases into the air on several occasions. The newspapers were full of photos, and all the television stations ran footage of these eruptions.

Each time it happened, Vicky begged her father and stepmother to drive the forty miles from their home in Longview, Washington, so she could see the volcano in person.

Vicky knew her father wanted to see the volcano up close just as much as she did. Every evening, when reports about Mount Saint Helens came on the television news, Mr. Huron leaned forward, listening to every word.

Every time there was a small eruption, Vicky got more excited.

Mrs. Huron got more nervous. When she heard the sheriff complain on television that tourists had removed barricades from roads in order to drive closer for a better look at the volcano, Mrs. Huron shook her head in disbelief. "Why would anyone in their right mind do that?" she asked. "Don't they know the roads are closed for good reason?"

Mrs. Huron had resisted the trip until that morning. Usually the whole family slept late on Sundays, but that day the Hurons' dog had barked frantically before daybreak, and everyone got up to see what all the noise was about. A cat lounged on the Hurons' patio, looking in the sliding glass door at the dog.

"Since we're up anyway," Vicky said

after they shooed the cat away, "and we don't have any plans for today, let's drive to Mount Saint Helens."

"Good idea," said Mr. Huron.

"No, thank you," said Mrs. Huron.

"This is our chance to witness history," Vicky said. "We may never get to see another active volcano. Some of the ash shot twenty thousand feet in the air."

"All the more reason to stay away," Mrs. Huron replied. "The paper yesterday said that more than fifteen hundred earthquakes have registered at Saint Helens in the last eight weeks."

"Wow!" said Vicky.

"The whole mountain has been declared an extreme hazard," Mrs. Huron continued. "Even the pilots of airplanes have been warned to stay at least thirty miles away."

"Most of those earthquakes were minor shakes," Mr. Huron said, "and they happened last month. There's been hardly any volcanic activity this week. There hasn't even been any ash for four days. I think the worst is over. If we wait any longer, we'll miss the show entirely. It may already be too late."

The Volcano Disaster

In the end Vicky and her dad won the argument.

Vicky's excitement increased as Mr. Huron drove toward Mount Saint Helens. "Look!" she said as she got her first glimpse of the top of the mountain. "I can see the crater."

"That's amazing," Mr. Huron said. He drove more slowly. "The last time we saw this mountain, it was a rounded, sloping white peak. That crater was formed the end of March."

"It really looks like a volcano now," Vicky said.

Mrs. Huron, who had reluctantly agreed to come along, kept her eyes on her knitting, as if hoping that if she ignored the mountain, it would do nothing to attract her attention.

"I'll bet we get some good pictures," Vicky said.

"The weather is cooperating," Mr. Huron said. "The mountain will show up better against blue skies than against clouds."

"When we get to the viewpoint, I'm going to aim my camera at the top of the mountain and wait," Vicky said. "Maybe I'll get lucky and a bunch of ash or smoke will blast out." She double-checked her camera, to be sure she had film in it. She also took it out of the carrying case and hung it around her neck, where she could grab it quickly.

Mr. Huron stepped on the brake, and Vicky looked to see why he was stopping.

Two sheriff's department cars stood nose to nose across the road, creating a roadblock.

Mr. Huron rolled down the driver's window and waited while a young man in uniform approached.

"I'm sorry, sir," the man said. "The road is closed from this point on."

Vicky scowled at the man.

"We want to drive to one of the viewpoints and take pictures of Mount Saint Helens," Mr. Huron said.

"It isn't safe to go any farther," the man replied. "The volcano could erupt at any time, and there would be no way for you to escape. All access roads are closed."

"Who made this decision?" Mr. Huron asked.

"The governor. Dixie Lee Ray."

"And who are you?" Mr. Huron asked.

"I'm with the National Guard, sir. We were called in to help. There were so many sightseers on this mountain, there was no way the local authorities could cope if there was a major eruption."

"There isn't going to be a major eruption," Mr. Huron said. "We'll be lucky to see any steam or ash at all."

"Nevertheless, the road is closed," the man said firmly.

"I have a right to drive where I want," Mr. Huron said. "These are public roads, and I pay taxes."

"My job is to protect the public," the man replied, "and right now it is not safe to go any closer to the volcano."

"There's no use arguing," Mrs. Huron said softly. "Just turn around and go home."

Mr. Huron turned the car around, but he didn't head for home. He drove about a mile and then stopped on the shoulder of the road, pulled a folded piece of paper from his pocket, and consulted it.

"What are you doing? What's that?" Mrs. Huron asked.

"It's a map of the Forest Service roads

that go into the Mount Saint Helens area. One of the guys at work was up here a couple of days ago. He said the major roads were blocked off then, too, but vendors in Castle Rock were selling copies of Forest Service maps so people could drive closer to Saint Helens on the smaller roads. He bought one of the maps, followed a logging road, and got some great close-up photos of the mountain."

"I hope you aren't intending to do anything so foolish," Mrs. Huron said. "If Governor Ray has closed the state roads to protect the public, then the public has no business going closer on some other route."

"It would be wimpy to go home now," Vicky said. "Dad's friend used the logging road, and nothing happened to him."

"It isn't wimpy to obey the law," Mrs. Huron said.

"Lots of people are using these back roads," Mr. Huron said.

"That doesn't mean it's safe," Mrs. Huron said.

"If I believed there was really any danger, I wouldn't want to do it, either," Mr. Huron said. "But you know how the government is—always making unnecessary rules for us when we are perfectly capable of deciding these matters for ourselves."

Mr. Huron laid the map on his lap and pulled back onto the road. Half a mile later he turned left onto an unmarked gravel road.

"You can stop right here and let me and Vicky out," Mrs. Huron said. "If the governor and the National Guard say it isn't safe to go closer, then I am not continuing on some back road."

Mr. Huron took his foot off the gas pedal. "I promise to be careful," he said as the car slowed. "We'll stay close to the car, and if the volcano starts to erupt, we'll hop in and drive away."

"Please?" Vicky said. "We'll never have another chance like this."

A station wagon carrying four teenagers passed them, headed toward the mountain.

"Other people are using this road," Vicky said.

"Well, we aren't," Mrs. Huron said.

"Let's drive just a bit farther," Mr. Huron said. "We should have a great view as soon as we get above these trees."

"If we don't go," Vicky said, "I'll be the only kid in my whole school who hasn't seen the volcano. I'll probably flunk out of ninth grade."

"It *is* an educational opportunity," Mr. Huron said.

"Five miles," Mrs. Huron said. "Five more miles, and then we turn around."

CHAPTER

6

As Warren looked at Mount Saint Helens, his first reaction was pure elation. The Instant Commuter worked!

I did it! Warren thought. I traveled through space, just the way Grandpa envisioned. When the probe touched the photo, it went into action, the same as it would if it touched a map. This was great! It opened up even more potential uses for the invention.

He looked up at the mountain again. It was a rounded peak except for the very top, which was indented. Apprehension nibbled around the edges of his excitement. Wasn't Mount Saint Helens more uneven in shape than that?

Warren tried to remember exactly what Mount Saint Helens looked like. He thought the crater was huge and irregular, where part of the side of the mountain had blown out during the eruption. But he wasn't sure.

Warren wished he had read all of the library book he had checked out about the volcano instead of just the first paragraph.

Until Mr. Munson assigned this topic, Warren had never had any reason to pay special attention to Mount Saint Helens. Mount Rainier, which was also part of the Cascade range, was the closest mountain to Issaquah, where Warren lived. He often saw Mount Rainier and knew exactly what it looked like. Once in a while, on clear days, he also glimpsed Mount Baker, to the north.

He had seen Mount Saint Helens only on the rare occasions when his family drove south to Portland, or east to Yakima, and then it was from a distance. Dad had always wanted to stop at the Mount Saint Helens Visitor Center on one of the trips south, but there had never been enough time.

Now he will never go there, Warren

thought, and the familiar sharp pang of grief made his chest feel tight. He pushed the feeling aside and looked at the mountain.

Although the shape didn't seem right to him, he decided he must be standing near Mount Saint Helens because that photo was the only thing the probe had touched.

A new idea jumped into his mind. Maybe the mountain was still cone-shaped, with only a small crater, because it had not yet erupted. Had he traveled through *time* as well as through space? Had he somehow journeyed not only to the place of the photo, but to the day when it was taken? Was he looking at Mount Saint Helens before the big eruption?

If so, how much before?

Was the volcano going to explode at any minute, with him standing there watching it?

Despite the warm sunshine, Warren felt chilled. I should have left the Instant Commuter on my back, he thought. At the time he had hoped that if he took it off, the machine would not have any further effect on him, and he would stay where he was.

But he had been too late. His trip had already started before he got the Instant

Commuter off. Once the process began, it did not stop no matter what happened to the Instant Commuter.

Now Betsy had the Instant Commuter, while Warren stood at the base of an active volcano, unsure whether it had already erupted or was going to erupt soon.

I have no way to get home, Warren thought. Without the Instant Commuter, I can't go back.

He wished he had told Betsy what he was doing. He wished he had shown her the Instant Commuter and explained what it was supposed to do. If he had, she might be able to figure out where he was. As it was, nobody knew.

Would Betsy tell them what had happened? If she did, would anyone believe her?

Gram might think he ran away or was kidnapped. And Mom. If Warren failed to return, poor Mom, who was still crying over Dad, would probably drop out of college and grieve all over again.

Stop it, Warren told himself. You'll get back home. All you have to do is run until you come to a town. Find a phone and call Mom.

The waffles moved uneasily in Warren's stomach.

When he first decided to use the Instant Commuter, he had known that if anything ever went wrong with the machine, and he needed a way to get home, he could always call Mom and she would come to get him. He could call her now, if he had only traveled through space, from one location to another.

But what if I traveled through time as well as space? Warren thought. If the mountain has not yet erupted, it is no later than 1980, long before I was born.

Warren did some quick arithmetic. Mom was only sixteen years old in 1980. Even if he knew how to reach her, which he did not, she was not likely to believe that she had a twelve-year-old son who was in trouble.

I can't call Mom, Warren thought, and without the Instant Commuter, I'm stuck here. I have no way to get back. Ever.

Warren's apprehension turned into full-blown panic. He wiped his hands on his jeans and looked at the mountain again. The snow at the top and on the slopes was not white, the way snow on a mountain-top usually is. This snow was a dingy gray color.

Gray. The color of volcanic ash.

Maybe it has already erupted, Warren thought. Maybe I'm wrong about the irregular shape. Maybe I didn't travel through time.

He couldn't stand there and wonder about it. If the volcano was about to blow up, he needed to get as far away from it as he could. If he had moved through space, but not time, he needed to find a telephone so he could call Mom. He walked along the gravel road, away from the mountain.

Weeds and grass grew up through the gravel; clearly, the road was not used much. The air was still, as if the whole world was holding its breath, waiting for something to happen.

Warren walked faster. The possibilities of where he was and what might happen to him ran rapidly through his mind like a videotape on fast-forward.

The silence was broken by a faraway sound. An engine? Warren's heart raced as he listened. Yes, it sounded like a car. A car was driving toward him.

Seconds later a station wagon barreled

toward him, leaving a cloud of dust behind it. Warren stood at the side of the road and waved his hands back and forth in front of his chest. He would ask the occupant of the vehicle to tell him the date—and to give him a ride to the nearest town.

The station wagon did not slow down.

"Hey!" Warren yelled as it reached him. "Stop! I need help!"

The station wagon kept going. Warren saw four teenagers inside. They laughed and pointed at Warren as they drove by. One tossed an empty beer bottle out the window.

Dust from the station wagon's tires blew into Warren's face. He turned away and followed the road again. What jerks, he thought. I hope they get fined for littering.

Ten minutes later Warren came to a barricade across the road and realized the kids in the station wagon had driven around it. Maybe they'll get fined for littering *and* arrested for trespassing, Warren thought. It would serve them right.

A red car approached, driving slowly on the gravel road. When it reached the barricade, it stopped. An orange sign on the barricade said ROAD CLOSED.

Warren hurried toward the car.

A man was driving. A woman rode in the front passenger seat, and a girl about fifteen years old sat in the backseat. As Warren got close enough to hear their voices, he realized that the man and the woman were arguing.

"I am not going around that barricade," Mrs. Huron said. "Vicky and I are getting out. Now." She opened the door. "Come on, Vicky," she said as she got out of the car. "We'll walk home if we have to."

"I want to go with Dad," Vicky said.

"Excuse me," Warren said as he approached the car.

All three people turned to look at him.

"Can you tell me today's date?" Warren asked.

"It's May eighteenth," Mrs. Huron replied.

Warren felt as if he had been punched in the stomach. When he got out of bed that morning, it had been January tenth.

"What year?" Warren asked.

Vicky snickered.

"I know this sounds kind of crazy," Warren said, "but I really need to know what year this is."

"It's 1980," Mrs. Huron said.

Vicky got out of the car and looked curiously at Warren. "Do you have amnesia or something?" she asked.

"This is May eighteenth, 1980?" Warren said.

"That's right," Mrs. Huron said, but her voice sounded suspicious now, as if she wondered what was wrong with Warren.

Mr. Huron turned off the engine and got out, too, standing close to his wife and daughter as if he feared Warren was about to attack them.

Warren pointed to the mountain. "Is that Mount Saint Helens?" he asked.

"Well, duh," said Vicky.

"It is," said Mrs. Huron.

Warren tried to picture the assignment paper that Mr. Munson had given him. It had stated the date of the eruption. What, exactly, had it said? At the time Warren had been so dismayed to discover that he had Betsy for a partner that he hadn't read the rest of the paper closely. But he thought it said "The Eruption of Mt. Saint Helens. May 18, 1980."

Yes, he was positive that's what it said.

May 18, 1980.

Today.

I did travel through time, Warren thought, and now I'm next to an active volcano that might as well be a ticking time bomb.

"Mount Saint Helens is going to erupt," Warren said.

"Oh, big news," said Vicky. "It's been erupting off and on for almost two months. Why do you think we're here?"

"Those were minor eruptions," Warren said. "Today is the major one."

The three people stared at him.

"What time is it?" Warren asked.

Vicky looked at her watch. "It's seven forty-five," she said, and then added, "in the morning, in case you don't know whether it's day or night."

Warren reset his watch to seven forty-five.

"Let's go," said Mr. Huron. "I want to get some pictures before the sun is too bright."

"Yes," said Vicky. She looked at Warren and spoke sarcastically. "We want to get some pictures of this huge eruption that's going to happen today." Clearly, she did not think he knew what he was talking about.

"Please believe me," Warren said. "You

54

need to get out of here. This volcano is going to blow up big time and it's going to happen today. This morning." He tried to recall the one paragraph he had read in the library book. "I can't remember the exact minute, but I think it was around eight-thirty."

"Was?" said Vicky. "You talk as if the eruption has already happened."

"It has," Warren said. "I mean—look, I'll explain later. Right now we need to get as far away as we can, because if we're still standing here when the mountain blows, we're going to be buried alive."

The two adults glanced at each other uneasily.

"You're weird," said Vicky.

"How can you predict an eruption, when the geologists can't?" said Mr. Huron.

"It's going to be a bigger explosion than a hydrogen bomb," Warren said. "Volcanic ash will blow across the whole United States."

"We're wasting time," said Mr. Huron. "Let's go."

"What if he's right?" Mrs. Huron said. "Maybe he's some sort of guardian angel, sent to warn us."

"I know I sound goofy," Warren said, "but you have to believe me. Mount Saint Helens is going to blow up this morning, and it's going to be way worse than anyone expects it to be."

Vicky stuck her hands in her armpits and flapped her elbows up and down like chicken wings. "The sky is falling! The sky is falling!" she said. "Cluck, cluck, cluck!"

"Please!" Warren begged. "You need to go back." He stepped toward the car. "And please take me with you."

"Are you alone?" Mrs. Huron asked.

"Yes."

"How did you get here?"

"I—walked."

"We're miles from any town."

"Rhonda," said Mr. Huron, "and Vicky, get in the car. We have better things to do than listen to a wacky kid predict the end of the world." He got behind the wheel and closed the door.

"It won't be the end of the world," Warren said, "but unless we get out of here fast, it will be the end of you. And me."

Vicky got in the backseat.

Mrs. Huron hesitated, looking at Warren.

Mr. Huron started the engine. He tapped the horn once.

Mrs. Huron jumped at the sound of the horn. Then she, too, got in the red sedan.

"Wait!" Warren cried. "You'll be crushed under the mud flow. You'll die on the mountain!"

The car moved forward. Instead of making a U-turn, as Warren hoped, Mr. Huron drove around the barricade.

As soon as the car was on the other side, it picked up speed. Bits of gravel flew out from under the tires as the Huron family headed closer to Mount Saint Helens. Vicky looked out the rear window, grinning broadly, and waved both hands at Warren.

You're going to die in less than an hour, Warren thought as he watched the car drive off.

And if I don't get out of here, I'll die, too.

He turned his back to the mountain and began to run.

CHAPTER

7

"Warren?" Betsy whispered. "Are you here? Are you invisible?"

Warren didn't answer.

Betsy knelt on the floor of Warren's bedroom. Her hands shook as she reached for the backpack that Warren had been wearing. She wasn't sure she wanted to touch it. She didn't want to disappear, the way Warren had.

Creampuff sniffed the backpack and whined. She sniffed the floor where Warren had stood, and whined some more.

"I don't understand it, either," Betsy said. "Where did he go? How did he vanish?"

Creampuff yipped once.

Betsy petted the dog and kept talking, hoping her voice would calm Creampuff. "Just before he disappeared, he tried hard to get this backpack off," Betsy said. "It's as if he knew something terrible was going to happen, and he wanted to prevent it."

Warren had held what looked like a large pencil, or a pointer, in one hand. Just before he disappeared, he had thrown the pointer on the floor.

Betsy looked at the pointer, noticing that a wire extended from the blunt end. She tapped the pointer lightly with one fingertip, and then quickly withdrew her hand, as if expecting to be burned. Nothing happened.

Encouraged, Betsy picked up the pointer and looked at it closely. Small blue letters on the yellow background said, "Probe."

She put the probe down and examined the backpack. A thin electrical cord drooped from one corner of the backpack, and Betsy saw that, until Warren had pulled it loose, the cord had been connected to the pointer.

She opened the backpack and looked inside. It was a machine of some kind, in a plain oblong box.

An On/Off switch on the top of the box was pushed Off. Since the machine was turned off, she hoped it would be safe for her to pick up the box and try to figure out what it was.

She slid the box out of the backpack, onto the floor. The box was built of thin balsa wood, the kind used for building model rockets. Two tiny brass hinges connected the top of the box to the back side. A small sliding bolt on the front opened smoothly. Betsy lifted the lid and peeked inside.

The tangle of wires and parts looked like the inside of a computer. It also looked like the diagram that was on Warren's table. She picked up the whole contraption, surprised by how light it was, and laid it next to the diagram. Then she compared the real thing with the drawing.

One corner of the box was dented in where it had hit the floor, and some loose wires dangled from the bottom, but the machine matched the diagram. An Instant Commuter.

Betsy had never heard of an Instant Commuter, but whatever it was, it had made Warren disappear.

Betsy picked up the thick notebook labeled Instant Commuter and began to read. She skimmed quickly through the material, but the more she read, the more incredulous she became.

If this invention worked the way it was supposed to, it would be the biggest news since men first walked on the moon. She looked at all of the drawings and compared each one with the written explanations in the notebook.

No wonder Warren had not wanted to get together with her to work on their report. She wouldn't want to take time to read about the eruption of Mount Saint Helens, either, if she was making an exciting invention like this one.

Betsy relaxed a bit. Warren had obviously been working on this project for a long time. He probably knew exactly what he was doing. She had thought he looked scared when he ripped the backpack off, but maybe he had tried to take it off because he didn't want to vanish in front of her.

Betsy wondered where Warren had gone. And when he would return.

The notebook said that the person wearing the Instant Commuter would immediately go to any place on a map that the tip of the probe touched. Warren had been holding the probe when he vanished. What map had the pointer touched?

Betsy looked at the table. A map lay to the right of the large diagram. She looked closer and recognized a map of King County. She noticed the circle around Pine Lake Middle School. Warren must have traveled to school, Betsy thought. He had gone to the school, and he was there right now, wondering how to explain to Betsy what had happened.

Betsy tried to convince herself that this is what had happened, but she couldn't quite accept her own reasoning.

Something wasn't right, Betsy thought. Warren was too panicky before he disappeared. When this machine started to work, he acted scared stiff. He had ripped it off as if it were a keg of dynamite with a lighted fuse.

Why? If he didn't want to vanish in front of me, he didn't have to touch the map. He could simply have turned the Instant Commuter off while I was here, and I would never have known anything about it.

What had happened? What went wrong?

She closed her eyes, remembering exactly what Warren had done. When she entered the room, Warren was standing in front of the King County map that showed Pine Lake Middle School. But he had moved when she came in. While they talked, he stood at the center of the table, in front of the diagram.

Betsy had noticed the diagram and tried to see what it was, but he had blocked her view. He kept his hand, the one holding the probe, behind his back, so she couldn't see it.

When Warren disappeared, the end of the probe had not been anywhere near the map. It had been near . . .

Oh, no. Betsy's eyes flew open as she remembered the final moments before Warren vanished. The probe must have touched the magazine.

According to the directions, the person wearing the Instant Commuter would be transported to the spot that the probe touched on a map. It must work with photos, as well. Warren probably didn't know about that ability, since there was no mention of it in the notebook.

That would explain why Warren got so

panicky and tried to take the Instant Commuter off. He knew, when the machine began to work, that he had not touched the map of Pine Lake Middle School. He had touched the photo of Mount Saint Helens, and he was not prepared to climb a mountain.

Quickly Betsy read the rest of the notebook entries. She came to the page that warned about taking a map along so you could get back home again.

Betsy gasped. It didn't matter whether Warren had a return map with him or not, because he was no longer wearing the Instant Commuter. Warren was more than a hundred miles away, and he had no way to get home.

She debated what to do. Should she tell Warren's grandma what had happened? She could imagine the panic if she went downstairs and announced to the book discussion group that Mrs. Spalding's grandson had disappeared and was probably somewhere on Mount Saint Helens.

Surely Warren will call, Betsy thought. He'll get to a telephone and call his grandma, and she'll make arrangements for him to return home.

The Volcano Disaster

But what if Warren wasn't anywhere near a phone? Mount Saint Helens was a huge mountain, in the middle of a wilderness area.

If Warren had landed at the Visitor Center, or someplace else where there were people, he would be fine. But what if he had plopped down halfway up the mountain? He could be miles and miles from a telephone. It would be easy to get lost if he wasn't near a trail. He could wander for weeks and not find his way out.

It might be cold up there, Betsy thought, and Warren wasn't wearing a jacket or gloves. If he landed near the summit, he would be in snow and ice. He could get frostbite, and if he was in the freezing cold too long, gangrene could set in.

Betsy remembered a medical book that showed pictures of a patient's toes where gangrene had set in as a result of frostbite. The toes had to be amputated.

Warren could lose his toes and fingers. Even worse, he could freeze to death.

Betsy decided to tell her parents what had happened. She looked around Warren's room, hoping to see a telephone. There wasn't one.

"Come on, Creampuff," she said. "We need to tell Mom and Dad what happened."

She led the chubby dog downstairs and slipped out the kitchen door without disturbing the book discussion group.

Betsy ran home. "Mom!" she yelled as she dashed in the door. "Dad! Lori!"

No answer. Betsy saw a note on the kitchen counter.

Hi, Bets, Mom's handwriting said. *We've gone to watch Lori's soccer game. Home about 2:30.*

It was only noon, and there was no way to contact her parents at her sister's soccer game. She took the leash off Creampuff and picked up the phone. She pushed 911 and, when the emergency operator answered, she said, "I think my friend is somewhere on Mount Saint Helens, but I don't know where. Can you send a search party to look for him?"

"Is he alone?" the operator asked. "Did he sign out at one of the designated hiking areas? Where did he start hiking from? How long has he been missing?"

The more questions she got, the more Betsy realized her answers were not satisfactory. Warren was alone, she said, but he hadn't signed out anywhere. She didn't know where on the mountain he was, and he had been missing only fifteen minutes.

"How did he get to Mount Saint Helens?" the operator asked. "Who drove him?"

"Nobody," Betsy said. "He made this invention called an Instant Commuter, and it lets you travel through space when you wear it on your back, and Warren meant to go to our school, but the probe touched a magazine photo of Mount Saint Helens by mistake, and then Warren vanished."

There was silence at the other end of the line. "If you think this is funny," the operator said, "you are mistaken."

"It isn't a joke!" Betsy said. "He's really gone."

"Let me speak to one of your parents," the operator said.

"They aren't home."

"I didn't think so. If you make a prank call to nine-one-one again, you'll be reported to the authorities."

The line went dead.

Betsy decided to go back and tell Warren's grandma. Maybe Mrs. Spalding knew all about the Instant Commuter. Maybe there was a way for Warren to get home even without the machine.

Leaving Creampuff at home, Betsy hurried back down the street and knocked on Mrs. Spalding's front door. Nobody answered.

She tried to open the door. It was locked.

She ran around to the back of the house and tried the kitchen door. It opened. "Hello?" she called, but no one answered. When she went inside, the rooms were empty.

The plates still sat on the dining room table, where Mrs. Spalding and her three friends had eaten lunch. A printed agenda lay on the table. Betsy picked it up and read it.

Children's Literature Discussion Group
11:00 Brunch and book discussion
12:30 Visit Woodland Park Zoo to see places
      mentioned in *Terror at the Zoo*
 4:00 Selection of next month's book

They've left for the afternoon, Betsy realized. They've gone to Seattle, and they won't return for almost three hours.

She climbed the stairs to Warren's room.

The Volcano Disaster

She didn't know how to help Warren, but she had to try something. She couldn't just go home and act as if nothing had happened. Maybe if she read the rest of the Instant Commuter information she would get an idea.

She sat in the chair by Warren's worktable and reached for the notebook. She noticed the magazine she had brought over and picked it up instead. It was still open to the photograph that Warren had accidentally touched with his probe.

Betsy read the caption under the photo: *Ash from prior eruptions girds the crater as Mount Saint Helens prepares to blow. Photo taken one hour before the May 18 eruption.*

A chill crept down Betsy's arms and legs. Was it possible, she wondered, for Warren to travel to the time of the photo, as well as the place? Was he trapped on Mount Saint Helens just as the volcano was going to erupt?

If so, Betsy had one hour from the time Warren vanished to figure out a way to get him back. She estimated that at least forty-five minutes were already gone. It had taken a while to read the notebook and look at the drawings. And she had gone home and come back.

Fifteen minutes. That's all the time she had to save him.

Even if she could convince anyone that Warren needed help, fifteen minutes was not enough time to send a rescue team. And she couldn't send a rescue team to a past year, anyway.

I'll have to do it myself, Betsy thought.

She flipped through the notebook to the page that showed the weight limit. "The Instant Commuter will carry anyone weighing 250 pounds or less," it said.

Betsy weighed eighty-six pounds. She didn't know how much Warren weighed, but he was about her height, and kind of skinny. Both of them together should be less than 250 pounds.

If she could get the Instant Commuter to work, she would touch the photo with the probe and go to Mount Saint Helens herself. And then she and Warren could lock arms and travel home together.

If she could get the Instant Commuter to work.

Betsy looked at the dented end of the box. She picked up one of the loose wires, consulted the diagrams, and reached inside the machine.

Carefully she attached the wire where she thought it belonged. As she worked, she heard the steady tick-tick-ticking of the clock on the table beside Warren's bed. Thirteen minutes, thirteen minutes, thirteen minutes, it seemed to say.

Twelve, twelve, twelve.

CHAPTER

8

"Nutty kid," Mr. Huron said as he drove away from Warren. "Why is he here, if he's so certain the mountain's going to erupt today?"

"He probably thinks it's cool to scare people," Vicky said. "What a flea brain."

"Stop the car," said Mrs. Huron.

Mr. Huron did. "Now what?" he demanded.

Mrs. Huron unbuckled her seat belt, then opened her door. "I'm going back," she said. "I didn't want to come in the first place, and even though I admit that boy said some strange things, there was something honest about him. I believe him. You can go on if you like; Vicky and I will walk back to the main road and ask one of the National Guard people for a ride."

"For Pete's sake," Mr. Huron said. "You're being totally irrational about this."

"Get out, Vicky," Mrs. Huron said.

"I don't want to get out," Vicky whined. "Do I have to?"

"No," said Mr. Huron. "You don't have to. This is ridiculous."

Vicky looked back and forth between the two adults.

"She's old enough to decide for herself," Mr. Huron said, "and she wants to go with me. If you insist on staying here, we'll pick you up in two hours."

"You'll be sorry if you don't come," Vicky said. "This might be your only chance to see a live volcano."

Mrs. Huron shook her head. "This might be my only chance to save my own life," she said. She got out of the car and shut the door.

"Maybe we should go back, too," Mr. Huron said. "I don't like leaving her."

"Dad!" Vicky said. "You promised!"

The car moved forward again.

Mrs. Huron's eyes filled with tears. "Be

careful," she whispered. She watched the red sedan until it rounded a curve and was out of sight. Then she turned and walked briskly in the other direction. When she reached the barricade, she looked around for the boy who had warned them to turn back. He was not there.

Maybe he really was an angel, Mrs. Huron thought. She had heard that angels sometimes appear—looking for all the world like ordinary mortals—and then, after they've saved the life of the person they came to help, the angels vanish.

Or maybe the boy just took his own advice and was headed down the mountain to safety. Mrs. Huron hoped that was the case, because if the boy was really an angel who had come to caution them, it meant that Mrs. Huron's husband and stepdaughter were driving straight toward disaster.

Mrs. Huron walked faster and faster, and finally broke into a run. If she could catch up to the boy, she would know he was only a kid, not a heavenly messenger warning her of impending doom.

Half a mile ahead of Mrs. Huron, Warren's mind churned even faster than his legs as he ran along the gravel road, trying to think what to do. Sweat ran down the back of his neck; his T-shirt stuck to his back.

How was he going to get home? Without the Instant Commuter, how could he travel forward in time to the place and year he had left?

Mom and Gram will think I ran away, Warren thought. They'll be frantic. They'll call the police.

If Betsy tells them I was wearing the Instant Commuter, and they figure out that it worked, and they look for me at Mount Saint Helens, they won't find me. Even if they search here, in this exact spot, they'll be years and years too late.

Warren looked at the time: eight-oh-one.

What have I done? he wondered.

Warren kept running as he fought back the panic and tried to figure out a way to get back home.

Maybe, he thought, I can build another Instant Commuter. Yes. Yes, that was his only chance.

He hoped he could do it. He had studied all the drawings and notebook pages many times; he might be able to remember them.

If he made it safely away from the volcano, and if he could somehow get the parts and tools he needed, he would try to build another Instant Commuter. Thank goodness he still had the map of home in his pocket. If he was able to make another machine, and get it to work, he should be able to return to Gram's house.

If this; if that. There are way too many *ifs* in my plan, Warren thought.

A sudden loud noise made him jump. He looked back at the volcano. Only the crater was visible now over the trees; it was unchanged. No smoke. No ash.

The noise continued, and Warren realized it was a chain saw in the woods off to his left. He rounded a curve in the road and saw a parked logging truck.

Warren slowed his pace. If loggers were allowed to come here to work, it must not be too dangerous. Or had the loggers, like the teenagers and the couple in the red car, driven around barricades and come in illegally?

When he reached the truck he stopped running and looked into the thick stand of trees, toward the noise. Although the whine of the chain saw was louder now, Warren saw no people.

Should he keep running, or should he find the loggers and talk to them? If he tried to tell them that the volcano was going to erupt any minute, they would probably react the same way the people in the red car had reacted. They wouldn't believe him. They would continue working, while he would have lost valuable time.

On the other hand, if they did believe him, he might be able to save their lives. Knowing what he did, he couldn't just go on without warning them.

Warren detoured into the forest, following the noise of the saw.

When the noise stopped briefly, he called, "Hello! I need to talk to you!"

Two men came toward him out of the trees.

"The volcano is going to erupt," Warren said.

"We have permission from the sheriff to be here," one man said. "We signed the papers saying we're responsible for ourselves."

"You don't understand," Warren said. "It's going to erupt today—this morning."

"We've heard that every day for weeks,"

the second man said. He gave Warren a suspicious look. "Who sent you?" he asked. "Did the sheriff send you?"

"He's a kid," the first man said. "The sheriff wouldn't send a kid."

"Nobody sent me," Warren said. "I just wanted to warn you."

"Thanks," the first man said, "but we're staying."

"You said you got permission to be here," Warren said. "Does that mean this area is considered dangerous?"

"Are you kidding?" the second man said. "Where have you been the last few weeks?"

Warren didn't answer.

"The whole county is considered a danger zone," the first man said. "If the sheriff had his way, nobody would come near this mountain, not even the geologists with their fancy equipment. But we're eighteen miles away from the summit at this point, and if we don't work, we don't get paid."

The two men turned to go back to their job.

Warren returned to the gravel road and kept running. The forest thinned and gave way to a meadow. The road, which had been downhill until then, flattened out for a while and then began to climb again.

The hill slowed Warren down and made the backs of his legs ache. He trotted more slowly, feeling short of breath. He tried to think of a way to get home that would be faster than building a whole new Instant Commuter.

Before he could think of one, he reached the top of a ridge. He stopped running, and looked back. He could see more of the mountain from here than he could when he was in the midst of the big trees. The sun was higher now, shining brightly on the mountain slopes. If he weren't so worried, he would enjoy the spectacular scenery.

The nearness of the mountain dismayed him. The loggers had said eighteen miles, and Warren had run some more since then, but Mount Saint Helens seemed close. Dangerously close.

He checked the time again. Eight twenty-nine. Except for the few minutes talking to the loggers, he had been running for almost forty-five minutes, and Mount Saint Helens looked just as close now as it had when he started. He still didn't see any signs of an eruption, but he knew it would happen soon.

Wearily Warren crossed the top of the ridge and continued to run. What else could he do? His only hope of escape was to get far enough away before the volcanic flow cascaded down the slopes.

He thought of his dad as he ran. In the months since the accident, Warren had felt life was not worth living. What was the use of trying, when you could get wiped out in one second by some fool who drank too much and then climbed behind the wheel of a car? Why bother to study, when you might not even be on earth the next day?

The challenge of making the Instant Commuter work had given Warren a reason to get up each morning, but his former enthusiasm for school, and sports, and for his friends had not returned.

But now, racing against what he knew was certain destruction, Warren wanted to live. He wanted to make the most of his life, while he could. He wanted to start studying again and bring his sagging grades back to where they used to be. He wondered if it was too late to go out for basketball. If it was, maybe he'd try track this year. He'd see if Skipper wanted to spend an afternoon playing Ping-Pong, or building model rockets. He'd even call Betsy and arrange to work on their report.

But first, he had to get home.

Faster, he told his legs. Go faster.

I want to live!

CHAPTER

9

The clock in Warren's room ticked on. Five minutes, five minutes, five minutes.

Betsy tried not to hear it, but no matter how hard she concentrated on fixing the Instant Commuter, she was always aware of the minutes racing by, and she kept glancing at the clock to see how much time she had left.

By the time Betsy connected the last dangling wire to where the diagram showed it should go, her head ached. She sat back and closed her eyes briefly.

Betsy didn't like mechanical things. She had never built models or taken apart her toys to see how they worked. Given an option, she would not have chosen to repair the Instant Commuter.

Today, there was no choice. There was no time to wait for help. Not if Warren was somewhere on the slopes of Mount Saint Helens.

If he had traveled through time, the volcano was about to blow. If he had traveled only through space, he could be freezing to death in the snow. Either way, Warren needed her help.

She wondered if he knew where he was. She wondered what year he was in. Most of all, she wondered if the repairs she had made to the machine would work.

There was only one way to find out. Betsy put the Instant Commuter into the backpack and pulled the probe out the opening. Then she put her arms through the straps and slipped the backpack on her back. She buckled the front strap across her chest.

She reached over her shoulder, and her fingers found the On switch. She hesitated.

Betsy's stomach felt the way it had before she went onstage for her piano recital.

Maybe I should leave a note, she thought.

If Warren's grandma comes home and he isn't here, she'll worry. And my parents will be frantic if they don't know where I am.

She wondered if Warren's grandma knew about the Instant Commuter and what it was supposed to do.

She found a blank piece of paper and a pencil. What should she say? If she left a note saying that she and Warren had used the Instant Commuter to travel to Mount Saint Helens, her family would freak out for sure.

Maybe a note wasn't necessary. If the repaired Instant Commuter worked, and she traveled to where Warren was and got him and they came home together, they would be back here before anyone found her note.

If the Instant Commuter didn't work, Betsy would stay right where she was, and she could explain in person what had happened to Warren. She put the pencil down.

Four minutes, four minutes, four minutes.

She reached for the On switch again. This time she pushed it.

She picked up the probe. She looked at the photo of Mount Saint Helens. Even if the machine worked, she knew she had a major problem. What part of the photo had the probe touched when Warren was holding it? The top? The middle? One edge?

Ideally, Betsy would put the probe on the same spot and appear right next to Warren. Despite her nervousness she smiled, thinking how surprised he would be if that happened.

However, the odds were good that she would *not* appear close to Warren. She could easily land miles away, with no way to find him.

If she touched the photo at the top of the mountain, she would end up on the rim of the crater. If she touched the photo at the bottom edge, she would be in a stand of large trees. Warren might be in either of those places, or anywhere in between.

I should take the photo with me, Betsy thought. If I can't find Warren after I get there, I will use the probe to touch the photo in a different place. I can keep moving myself around until I find him.

Three minutes, three minutes, three minutes.

Betsy ripped the photo out of the magazine. When she did, it uncovered another photo in the same article.

Betsy froze. The second picture was taken only two minutes before the eruption.

If Warren had traveled to the time of the first photo, Betsy thought, I should go to the time of the second one. The second picture was shot nearly an hour after the first one, and that's how much time has passed since Warren vanished.

She dropped the first page on the table and ripped the second photo out of the magazine. She held it in her left hand; with her right hand she aimed the tip of the probe at the middle of the second photograph.

Two minutes, two minutes, two minutes.

Betsy swallowed hard and touched the picture. The machine vibrated gently against her back.

It's working! Betsy thought. I fixed the Instant Commuter!

A strong wind blew her hair away from her face. Betsy grabbed the chair to keep her balance. As Warren had done, she closed her eyes against the wind. The wind lasted several seconds and then ended as abruptly as it had begun.

Betsy opened her eyes to sunlight. She squinted, waiting for her eyes to adjust to the brightness. I'm on Mount Saint Helens, she thought. I came one hundred miles in less than half a minute. What an incredible machine!

She stood on a rock, surrounded by gray snow. She turned in every direction, looking for Warren. Below her, in the distance, she saw a lake, and forests. She realized she was partway up the mountain. But was she still in the present—or had she gone back to 1980?

She cupped her hands around her mouth and shouted, "Warren!"

Her words vanished into the vast emptiness.

She shivered despite the sunshine. If Warren had landed in a barren area like this, he must be terrified. It was so cold here, and so desolate.

She called again. "Warren! Warren Spalding!"

Warren raced on.

Partway down the second ridge, he

looked at his watch again. Eight thirty-one. Maybe he had remembered the time wrong. Maybe the mountain didn't erupt at eight-thirty.

He stopped running and took a deep breath. He stuck his right foot out in front of him, straightened the leg and hung his head toward his knee, stretching out his tired leg muscles. He held the pose for a few seconds and then did the same thing with his left leg. While he stretched, he watched the mountain warily.

Just as he straightened up, the ground dropped from beneath his feet and he fell backward onto the gravel road. A low rumbling noise, like a faraway freight train coming through the forest, filled the air. Warren scrambled to his feet and looked back.

Sections of the top of the mountain were shifting downward. It was as if a huge knife had sliced through one side of the volcano, cutting three big pieces loose from the top. The pieces slid quickly, one after the other.

Too awestruck to run, Warren stared as the gigantic slabs moved down the side of the volcano. As they fell, a plume of steam rose from the top of the volcano. Almost immediately the steam turned dark.

It must be volcanic ash, Warren thought, or some sort of gas. It ballooned upward like an enormous black cauliflower, filling the sky. More ash came from the face of the landslide.

At the same time an even bigger cloud of ash and debris shot sideways out of the mountain, from the opening created when the pieces slid down. The volcano was erupting sideways, just as Betsy's article had said.

The clouds quickly merged into one huge mass as volcanic debris blasted from inside the volcano.

The ash plume was enormous, and when it mixed with the landslide debris, it became a thick, dark wind.

It's as if someone set off tons of dynamite inside the mountain, Warren thought. Instead of just one single blast, like a bomb would be, this was a sustained explosion that kept coming and coming. He wished he had brought his camera, but even without pictures Warren knew he would never forget this sight.

He also knew he could not stand and

watch any longer. He had already wasted precious seconds because he had been too shocked to react.

He turned and continued to race down the far side of the ridge. It was much hotter now than it had been before. He felt the heat on his back first, and then all around him. The ground seemed to burn through the bottom of Warren's shoes.

Splat! A mud ball landed beside him, splashing his jeans. Another mud ball landed on his shoulder. Warren cried out, and tried to shake the hot mud off his shirt without touching it. *Splat! Splat!* It was like being in a mammoth snowball fight, except these balls were scorching hot. There was no way to dodge them. Some landed in front of him, some behind, and some on either side.

One hit him right on top of the head. Warren bent over, shaking the mud out of his hair. His scalp felt burned; he touched his hair with his fingers, fearing he might have a bald spot where the mud ball had landed. His hair felt brittle, but it was still where it belonged.

He heard what he thought was someone else running. Looking over his shoulder, he saw a panicked deer bounding from the forest.

The sky grew dark, the way it did before a heavy rain, and then darker still. Ash dropped, quickly covering the road with a layer of gray. It was like running through newly fallen snow.

The old nursery song echoed crazily in Warren's mind: "Ring around the rosie, a pocket full of posies. Ashes, ashes, all fall down."

In less than five seconds the sky had gone from bright sunshine to total darkness. Flaming cinders rained down, sparking several small fires.

Fear made him run faster, his muscle aches forgotten.

Warren choked and coughed with every breath. What does volcanic ash do to human lungs? he wondered. Was inhaling it like smoking a thousand cigarettes? He bent his arm and buried his nose and mouth in his elbow, trying to breathe in as little ash as possible.

The air was black as a bowling ball; Warren could no longer see the road. The only light came from the burning cinders and the bolts of lightning which now zapped the air above him, one after another. Some of the lightning was orange; some was green, but Warren was too concerned about getting to safety to wonder about the colors.

The gravel beneath his feet felt as if it had just come out of a hot oven, like the warming stone that his mother put in the bottom of the bread basket, to keep dinner rolls warm.

Warren coughed harder.

Once, on a Boy Scout camping trip, Warren had stirred the campfire with a stick, to be sure it was out before he left. Smoke and ash had risen and filled his nostrils. This air smelled like the charred remains of that campfire, only this was worse. Here, he couldn't turn his head away and gulp in fresh air.

CHAPTER

10

Mrs. Huron, who did not run as fast as Warren did, arrived at the logging truck just as the eruption began.

Shocked by the earthquake, she stopped running and stared back at the volcano. The sky darkened and ash began to fall.

When the blast erupted sideways, Mrs. Huron watched, stunned, until its force reached her.

The hot wind threw stones and mud balls at her. Around her, tree trunks snapped like broken matchsticks. One tree landed across the top of the logging truck, smashing in the roof like a toy that was stomped on by a naughty child.

Turning in panic, Mrs. Huron stumbled and fell. When she landed, she heard a bone break near her left wrist. A sharp pain circled her arm.

One of the loggers crashed out of the woods behind her. He stopped when he saw the truck. "Oh, no!" he said.

He noticed Mrs. Huron on the ground and called, "Are you all right?"

"I broke my arm."

"My partner—" The logger choked on the words, cleared his throat, and tried again. "My partner was hit by a falling tree. He was gone before I could even get to him to try to cut him loose."

The earth shook again.

"Do you have a car?" the logger asked. "We need to get out of here."

"No."

"Then we'll have to run for it. Come on!" He extended a hand, to help her up.

Mrs. Huron shook her head. "I'll wait for my husband," she said. "I stayed behind while he and Vicky drove closer to the volcano. They'll return now to pick me up."

"If they went much closer," the logger said as he ran past her down the gravel road, "they might not come back."

The Volcano Disaster

The air grew black as midnight. Hot debris rained down.

"Run!" the logger yelled. He knew the woman was in shock and not thinking clearly. But he couldn't force her to move, and there wasn't time to argue.

If I make it out safely, he thought, I'll send someone back to help her.

Tears streamed down Mrs. Huron's cheeks as she watched the logger disappear, but she did not get up.

Balls of hot mud splashed down around her.

Holding her injured arm close to her side, Mrs. Huron looked down the road toward Mount Saint Helens. She hoped to see a red sedan. She saw only ash, and soon it was too dark to see at all.

Fearing for the safety of her family, Mrs. Huron stood, and ran after the logger.

The ash came up to Warren's ankles now. His eyes smarted. The smokey smell filled the inside of his head; his temples throbbed.

Unable to see where he was going, he tripped over a fallen tree. When his hands hit the ground, they were wrist-deep in tall grass; he realized he was no longer on the road. Crawling on his hands and knees, he dug his fingers through the ash until he felt gravel again. He had to stay on the road. If he didn't he could end up going in circles, completely disoriented, and he'd never find help.

If I was going to get buried by hot lava, Warren thought, it would have happened by now. I must have been far enough away from the crater, when it blew, to escape the lava flow.

Bright shards of lightning continued to slice through the blackness. A series of sharp earthquakes jolted the earth.

Breathing became more difficult.

He began to slide his feet forward, as if he wore Rollerblades or skis. It was easier than trying to lift his feet out of the thick ash for each step, and it helped him know he was still following the road.

No matter how he moved his feet, each movement caused the fallen ash to billow upward again. Besides breathing in what still fell from the sky, he was breathing the ash he stirred up by his own actions.

I've survived the actual blast, Warren

thought, but I might suffocate from the ash. After Dad's accident, everyone said what a tragedy it was that he died so young, only thirty-seven years old. But I'm just twelve. That's way too young to die.

If I do find my way back to other people, will I be able to build another Instant Commuter and make it work? Will I ever get home again?

He forced the gloomy thoughts out of his mind. "Think positive," Mom always said. "Every cloud has a silver lining."

Another streak of lightning briefly illuminated the area. Warren saw only ash on the ground, as far as he could see. All the grass and plants were covered, as if gray sheets had been draped over them.

It's like walking on the moon, he thought, except the astronauts' heads were protected by those plastic bubbles, and they breathed pure air.

Right foot. Left foot. Cough, cough, cough.

Maybe I should stop and wait for someone to find me, Warren thought. If I stood still, I wouldn't need to breathe so hard.

But would anyone find him? How could

they even look for survivors? Rescuers wouldn't be able to see any better than he could. And, besides, no one knew he was here. Search parties would look for people who were known to be in the vicinity, like the loggers.

That thought made Warren feel better. If a rescue team looked for those loggers, they might find Warren, too.

He wondered what had happened to the people in the red car. They had driven toward the volcano, and when it erupted, they had not come back.

No other roads had branched off the one he was on; it seemed to be the only way out. If the three people had been able to turn their car around in time and drive away from the blast, they would have reached him by now.

Warren had disliked the girl in the red car, but his chest tightened as he imagined her fate.

He coughed harder, gagging on the grayness.

"Warren!" Betsy called again.

As she listened for an answering shout,

the earth shook violently, knocking Betsy off her feet, onto the rock.

A deafening roar filled the air; the earth moved again.

I did travel through time, Betsy thought as she grabbed the probe. *And now Mount Saint Helens is blowing up! Right here! Right now! Right beneath me!*

Immediately, without taking time to get to her feet, Betsy touched the bottom left corner of the photo with the tip of the probe.

She felt the strong wind blow again.

At the same time an intense heat surrounded her, as if she were standing beside a roaring fire. Fearful that the magazine picture would go up in flames, she stuffed it in the pocket of her jeans. She covered her face with her hands.

The roar in her ears got louder. She had read enough about the eruption to know that the roar was the volcano shifting position, and the heat came from the volcanic gases that were released when the mountain moved. She knew that the hot gas and rocks from inside the volcano would shoot high into the air—and then fall back

to earth, destroying everything beneath
them.

Is the Instant Commuter fast enough to
get me away in time? she wondered. Will I
be gone before I'm burned to a crisp?

"Hurry!" Betsy yelled to the wind. *"Get
me out of here!"*

CHAPTER

11

This time the wind that accompanied the running of the Instant Commuter lasted only a few seconds. And this time, when Betsy opened her eyes, she was standing on the bank of a river.

The loud roar was gone, replaced by the sound of the water moving downstream.

The air was no longer hot, but Betsy remembered how the hair on her arms had felt singed, and the backs of her hands had been blistered. Another minute, she thought, and I would have looked like a marshmallow that dropped from the roasting stick into the fire.

Luckily, it had not taken as long the second time for her to travel from one place to the other. She wondered if that was because she didn't go as far. The first time, when she went from Warren's house in Issaquah to the slope of Mount Saint Helens, the wind had seemed to blow for about twenty seconds. This time, when she only went from the middle of the mountain to its base, the travel time was far less. Five seconds, perhaps.

Even so, that was close, Betsy thought. Much too close.

Her legs shook so hard that she could barely walk, but she forced herself to hurry to the edge of the river because she knew cold water is a good first-aid treatment for burns. She plunged her arms into the cold water and then splashed it on her face.

When she got up, she turned away from the river.

"Warren!" she called. "Warren Spalding! Can you hear me? Are you here?"

She saw a road ahead, but there were no cars and she saw no other people.

A sign on the road said NORTH FORK TOUTLE RIVER.

"Warren!" she yelled. "Warren, where are you?"

The Volcano Disaster

The air grew suddenly dark, as if a cloud had passed in front of the sun. Quickly it became darker still. She looked toward the river, and though she could still hear the water tumbling over the rocks as it ran downstream, she could no longer see it.

She couldn't see the sign, either. Within seconds she could barely see two feet in front of her face.

A bright streak of lightning crackled overhead.

She felt drops on her head and arms, as if it were raining, but the drops did not soak into her clothing, or into the ground.

It isn't rain, she realized. It's ash. I'm farther away from the actual blast than I was before, but my time has run out again.

She coughed as she inhaled the ash. Was it poisonous? she wondered. She pulled the neck of her T-shirt up over her nose and mouth, trying to filter the air while she quickly pulled the crumpled magazine page from her pocket. She held it close to her face, trying to see the photo in the darkness.

On her second trip she had traveled to the bottom left side of the photograph. This time she wanted the probe to touch the bottom right side. She squinted, trying to tell which was the top of the page and which was the bottom, but it was impossible to see.

Orange lightning licked through the black cloud like a snake's tongue. Even with the T-shirt over her face, she breathed in the thick ash.

Hoping she had the correct corner of the photo, she touched the probe to the page and felt the Instant Commuter quiver into action.

Betsy wondered where she would land. Wherever it was, she knew she would again go back to the time the photograph was taken, and when she got there, she would have only two minutes to find Warren before the volcano erupted.

Again, she felt the strong wind. Again, after only a few seconds, it stopped. Betsy opened her eyes.

The falling ash was gone. A different loud noise, that of an enormous engine, vibrated around her. She clapped her hands over her ears.

Betsy sat in a helicopter, looking down at a steaming gray wasteland. Something went wrong with the Instant Commuter, she thought. I'm looking at the volcano after the eruption, not before.

Betsy saw the pilot point out his window. The man who sat in the seat beside the pilot looked, and nodded.

Betsy looked, too. Far below, the top half of a car emerged from the ash. From the hubcaps down, the car was totally buried. The part that stuck up was covered with ash, too, but the outline of the vehicle was visible. Both doors on one side of the car were open, as if the driver and a backseat passenger had fled in a hurry.

The helicopter pilot hovered over the car, and Betsy realized he was going to land beside it.

As the helicopter dropped in altitude, the blades created a strong wind, which stirred up such thick clouds of ash that the pilot could no longer see. He had to abandon his plan to land. He went back up and tried again in a different spot, with the same result.

When the wind from the chopper blades temporarily blew the ash off the car, Betsy could tell that the car was red. A red sedan. It quickly became gray again as the helicopter rose and ash settled back over the car.

"I don't see any survivors!" the pilot shouted to his companion. "If the people ran from the car, they would not have gone far."

"How could anyone live through that?" the other man said. "It's like the end of the world down there. If we find anything, it will be bodies."

Betsy shuddered. She wondered who had been riding in the red car and why they had been on Mount Saint Helens. Were they scientists, or were they sightseers who had ignored the warnings to stay away?

Was Warren down there somewhere, buried under the ash?

The pilot and the other man, who both wore uniforms and earphones, stared intently out the front windows. They did not notice her behind them, and Betsy sat perfectly still, not wanting to attract their attention. It would be impossible to explain how she got there.

The helicopter flew on. Betsy looked down at dark rivers of mud and ash, still flowing from the crater. Fallen trees, stripped of their leaves or needles, lay like matches dumped from a matchbox.

There was no sign of life. Once she saw

what looked like animal tracks in the ash, but the tracks ended at a black mudhole.

The men were right, Betsy thought. No living thing could have survived this. If Warren was down there, it was too late for her to help him.

Wondering why she had landed after the eruption this time, she looked carefully at the wrinkled magazine page. She turned it over, to see what was on the other side, and realized what had happened. One side of the page was the photo taken just before the eruption; the other side was a different picture, taken the day after the eruption.

In the darkness of the falling ash, Betsy had held the magazine page with the wrong side up. She had put the probe on a different photo.

She read the caption on the second photo. "A National Guard Jet Ranger helicopter hunts for survivors on May 19. During its two-hour mission, the helicopter recovered the bodies of four teenagers who were overcome near their abandoned station wagon."

Betsy felt sick to her stomach. I'm leaving, she decided, before the National Guardsmen notice me. And before they bring dead bodies on board.

She turned the page over, to the photo she had intended to use all along. At least this time she could see what she was doing.

It may be too late anyway, she realized. No matter where Warren had landed, his time to escape was up.

Betsy was still able to jump back and forth in time because each time the probe touched the photo, she went back to the time when the picture was taken, two minutes before the eruption.

Warren couldn't do that. The picture Warren touched with the probe was taken an hour before the eruption. That hour was now gone for him.

Betsy hoped he had used the time to get himself to a safe place. If he had not, it didn't matter how long she searched for him. She would not find him alive.

I'll try one last time, Betsy decided. I'll go where I intended to go last time, to the bottom right corner of the pre-eruption photo. I can't take myself any closer to the top of the volcano, or I might not have enough time to get away. I'll touch the bottom right-hand side of the picture and see where I land.

If I'm still in danger there, I'll go home.

The Volcano Disaster

And that is when Betsy realized her big mistake.

She had read the warning in the notebook that said she should be sure to take a map of home with her. But in her haste to rescue Warren before the mountain exploded, she had forgotten about the map.

She had the Instant Commuter, and she had the magazine page with the two photos. But she had no map of home. Without a map, she was just as trapped in this time and place as Warren was.

CHAPTER

12

I could stay in the helicopter, Betsy thought. If I stay here, I know I won't be killed by the erupting volcano because we're flying on the day after. The danger is over.

But staying in the helicopter would mean staying in the year 1980, and Betsy didn't want to do that. She wanted to go home, to Mom and Dad and Lori. Even though she often argued with her sister, it was horrible to imagine not ever seeing Lori again.

And what about Warren?

Without the Instant Commuter, Betsy thought, Warren can't get home. Without Warren's map, I can't get home. He needs me, and I need him.

She decided to keep trying until she found him, even if it meant a dozen trips back and forth in space. She would put the probe on the photo, trying a different place on the picture each time. Sooner or later she would land near Warren.

A new fear filled her. The Instant Commuter ran on a battery, and the instructions had said to recharge it after each trip. How long would the battery last without being recharged? How many trips was it good for before it ran down? If it gave out, then neither she nor Warren would be able to go home.

Don't imagine disasters, Betsy told herself. Do what you can to solve the problem and don't worry about *what-ifs*.

She pointed the probe at the bottom right corner of the pre-eruption photo, touched the page, and closed her eyes, bracing herself for the wind.

This time the wind lasted only a few seconds. The noise of the helicopter engine ended abruptly. Betsy opened her eyes and looked around. She stood on the top of a hill; the ground sloped gradually down and then rose again. Beyond the second ridge, she saw Mount Saint Helens in the distance. Forest land began partway up the second ridge. Foothills, Betsy thought. I'm in the foothills area of the mountain range.

She cupped her hands around her mouth and shouted toward the mountain. "Warren! Warren Spalding!" Her voice floated across the treetops and disappeared into the gray patches of snow on the mountain slopes.

Turning in the other direction, she saw a clearing and, beyond the clearing, what looked like some sort of a road. She hurried toward it, calling as she ran. "Warren! Warren, are you here?"

If he had landed near here, Betsy decided, he would run away from the volcano when it erupted. She reached a narrow gravel road and followed it, hoping Warren might be somewhere ahead of her. A sense of urgency kept her moving quickly. She knew she had less than two minutes until the volcano erupted.

"Warren!" she cried. "Can you hear me?"

A sudden sharp jolt of the earth dropped Betsy to her knees. Here it goes again, she thought. She was farther away from the volcano this time, but she was just as scared.

She looked quickly at the magazine photo and decided exactly where she would touch it next with the probe. She put her finger on the spot and kept it there, pinching the page tightly between her thumb and forefinger. If she needed to leave in a hurry, she could.

The earth rumbled again. Looking back at the volcano, Betsy saw the dark cloud of volcanic gas and debris mushroom upward.

"Warren!" she yelled. "Where are you?"

Ash began to fall. As it had when she stood beside the river, the sky darkened quickly, and the ash grew thick. I'll stay as long as I can breathe, Betsy decided. I'll keep calling for Warren until I absolutely can't inhale any longer.

She decided to stay where she was, so she would need less oxygen. Warren could be behind her, rather than in front of her, so there wasn't much point in running.

Again, she pulled the neck of her shirt up to cover her nose and mouth, hoping the material would act as a filter and keep any harmful ash out of her nose.

Feeling as if she were viewing the end of the world, Betsy sat cross-legged in the middle of the gravel road and watched the gray sky turn black, while the ash got thicker and thicker.

Frequent forks of lightning gleamed overhead. Ash soon buried her shoes. A thick layer accumulated on her shoulders and her legs; she shook her head to keep it from piling up on her hair.

She counted. Every ten seconds, she pulled the shirt away from her mouth and shouted, "Warren!" Then she sat silently listening, hoping for a response.

If he was going to hear her, it needed to be soon. Betsy didn't think she could last much longer without fresh air.

Warren plowed forward, still sliding his feet so he stayed on the road. His eyes felt scratchy, as if he had strained them by reading too long in poor light. His back ached. With each step, he felt his energy seep through the soles of his shoes and soak into the ground.

He thought how good it would feel to rest—to lie down and let the blanket of ash cover him while he fell asleep.

His feet slid more slowly. Could he really save himself by going on, or was he simply unable to face facts? Maybe he should just give up, instead of struggling to survive. It would be so much easier to quit.

He stopped. A lone tear carved a path through the dusting of ash on Warren's cheek. He didn't bother to brush it away.

He wondered what Mom was doing. Studying, probably. Striving to make something good happen, to finish college and start a new career. I want to be there, Warren thought, cheering and clapping, when Mom gets her diploma. He moved forward again.

Slide, slide. Left foot, right foot.

Despite all the heartaches and disappointments in his life, he didn't want it to end. Not now. Not yet.

He moved faster again, his fists clenched with determination.

I will not quit! As long as I can move, I'll keep going.

Slide, slide.

Right foot, left foot, right foot.

Slide, slide, slide.

"Warren!"

Warren stopped. Had someone called his name, or was he imagining voices? He stood still, listening.

"Warren!"

Yes! There it was again. Someone was here! Someone was searching for him!

"Hello!" Warren shouted. "I hear you!"

When Betsy heard him respond, she leaped to her feet, causing a whirlwind of ash to swirl around her. Her arms tingled with excitement. His voice had come from behind her, toward the volcano, but she couldn't tell how far away he was.

"Keep calling!" she shouted. "Come this way!"

"Is it you, Betsy?" he yelled. "I'm coming! I'm on a gravel road!"

Betsy started toward his voice.

"Yes!" she shouted. "It's me. I'm on the road, too. Come this way!" She kept her shirt over her mouth. Even though it muffled her voice, it also prevented much of the ash from entering her nose and mouth.

Lightning flashed again.

Warren's legs, which moments earlier had felt too tired to take another step, surged forward faster and faster. Betsy's voice filled him with new energy, and fresh hope.

"I can't see anything," Warren called. "Keep talking." All the shouting, and the faster movement, increased his need for air.

He inhaled deeply and then coughed, a hard racking cough that made his chest hurt.

Once he started coughing, he couldn't stop. He was forced to breathe in through his mouth as well as his nose. When he inhaled at the end of one particularly painful cough, he swallowed a great gulp of scalding ash. It clogged his throat, and Warren began to choke.

"Warren!" Her voice sounded close now, but he couldn't get enough air to answer her. He choked and coughed, trying to rid his throat of ash, but taking in more with each breath.

Knowing that movement stirred up the ash, he stopped walking.

He doubled over, still choking, gasping for breath. He cupped his hands over his nose and mouth, trying to create a space where he could breathe without inhaling more ash.

Fighting for air, he felt light-headed. I'm going to pass out, Warren thought, and he dropped to the ground so he wouldn't get hurt when he fell.

The change of position sent blood to his head, which kept him from fainting. He lay on his side, propped up on one elbow, still choking, still trying to get the ash out of his throat. The inside of his mouth felt blistered from the hot ash.

"Warren? Where are you? Answer me!"

Warren could only gag helplessly and hope she would hear him.

CHAPTER

13

Thud.

Warren felt a sharp pain in the middle of his back, as if someone had kicked him right between his shoulder blades.

The sudden jolt jarred the ash in his throat loose; he spit it out.

Cough, cough, cough.

Warren still struggled for breath, but he was no longer in danger of choking. He felt a hand on his head; the fingers moved lightly across his hair as if a blind person was trying to decide what he was.

"Warren?"

In between coughs Warren managed to squeak, "Betsy?"

"It's me," Betsy said. "I'm sorry I kicked you."

Warren got to his feet. He could see only a dark outline where she stood, but he had never been so glad to hear a voice.

"How did you get here?" Warren gasped. "How did you know where I was?"

"I used the Instant Commuter," Betsy said. "Do you have a map of home?"

Warren took the map out of his shirt pocket and held it toward Betsy, waving it back and forth in the darkness until her hand found it.

Cough, cough.

"Hang on to me," Betsy said, and Warren realized what she planned to do.

Warren put his arms around her waist, feeling the hard lump of the backpack against his chest. The canvas was warm; he knew the Instant Commuter was still running. Could the small machine carry two people, he wondered, or would they overload its capacity and burn it out, leaving him and Betsy to choke on ash?

He clasped his fingers tightly together. He felt the movement of Betsy's arms as she touched the tip of the probe to the map.

Please, Warren thought. *Please take us home.*

The wind began to blow. Warren closed his eyes and held his breath. Betsy's hands gripped his arms. He knew she was trying to make sure he stayed with her.

The wind roared in his ears. It was working! Warren felt giddy with relief.

After a few seconds Warren took a tentative breath of air. It was plain air, clean air, and he took a deeper breath.

The wind stopped.

Warren opened his eyes and stepped away from Betsy.

They both looked around to see where they were. Familiar signs greeted them: Mail Post, Starbucks Coffee, Baskin-Robbins Ice Cream. Across the street they saw the back side of their school.

"We're in the parking lot of the Pine Lake Shopping Center," Betsy said. She sounded as relieved as Warren felt.

"Are you okay?" Warren asked.

"Yes. Are you?"

He nodded. "You saved my life," he said. He felt like hugging her, but he was too shy, even though he had just traveled over one hundred miles with his arms locked around her waist.

"My hands were burned," Betsy said, "but now they're fine. And there's no ash on our clothes."

"Now that we're home," Warren said, "it's as if we had never gone."

"This is one amazing machine," Betsy said. "How does it run? When did you make it? Did you know it would work on a picture?"

"No. And I didn't know it would take me backward in time."

"Let's go home," Betsy said, "and write down everything we saw, for our report."

"How can you think of school at a time like this?" Warren said. "We just escaped from the eruption of Mount Saint Helens. And we used, for the first time, an invention that's going to save the world from air pollution."

"What do *you* want to do?" Betsy asked.

"Eat. I haven't had any lunch, and I'm starving."

"Running away from a volcano works up an appetite," Betsy agreed.

They walked the ten blocks home, talking nonstop about what they had seen.

Gram and her book club friends weren't back yet.

Betsy called home and left a message on the answering machine so her parents would know where she was when they returned. Warren dished up the extra food from Gram's party.

"It's incredible," Warren said as he and Betsy ate fruit salad, sourdough bread, and brownies. "While Gram and her friends went to the zoo, and your sister played a soccer game, we've gone back to 1980 and lived through the eruption of Mount Saint Helens."

"Are you going to tell anyone what happened?" Betsy asked.

"Do you want to tell?"

"No."

"Neither do I," said Warren.

They smiled at each other, in the special way of friends who share a secret.

After they ate, they spent more than an hour writing down everything they had seen at Mount Saint Helens.

"I was putting off reading the library book I checked out," Warren said, "but now that I've been to the volcano, I want to read it, and the ones you took, too."

"I want to learn as much as I can about Mount Saint Helens."

When they got tired of writing, they started the video. They watched the cloud of ash rise into the air, knowing they were lucky to be alive.

"It was an amazing adventure," Warren said, "but I wouldn't want to do it more than once."

"I was there!" Betsy said, when the video showed aerial views, taken from a helicopter. "I saw that."

Thousands of trees lay like scattered toothpicks. The Toutle River, where Betsy had been, was clogged with mudflow from melting glaciers. The mudflow peaked at twenty-one feet high.

Flowing at thirty miles per hour, the muddy waters had quickly overflowed the banks, burying livestock and ruining houses. A lumber yard was washed away, creating huge logjams that snapped steel bridges in half.

More than one hundred fifty miles of trout and salmon streams, and twenty-six lakes, were destroyed by the eruption.

The video moved forward in time, showing new life where the destruction had seemed total. Within days of the eruption, small animals and insects returned to reclaim their territory. Plants such as lupine and fireweed soon grew up through the ash.

The desolate gray landscape gradually became green again, and the unexpected renewal of Nature was even more awesome than the volcanic eruption.

As Warren viewed the restoration of life where everything had seemed so dead, he felt the last traces of despair over Dad's accident drain away. He would always miss Dad, and remember him, but life no longer seemed pointless or hopeless.

Instead, he was exhilarated by his great plans for the future. On Monday, he would use the school's computer and look for information about Mount Saint Helens on the Internet. He would offer to help Betsy walk Creampuff. He would ask Mr. Munson if he could do an extra-credit project, to raise his grades.

Betsy's voice broke into his thoughts. "Gophers spend most of their lives underground," she said. "The word *gopher* comes from the French word for 'honeycomb,' referring to the underground tunnels the gophers make."

Warren blinked at her, wondering what in the world she was talking about. Then he realized the video had said some of the pocket gophers at Mount Saint Helens survived the eruption. That information had triggered Betsy's memory.

The video ended with shots of Mount Saint Helens as it is now. The huge crater remains surrounded by layers of ash, but the hardy wildflowers have spread into wide carpets of color. Thick forests climb the foothills once more; herds of elk and deer graze on lush green growth.

Trees have begun growing even in the inner blast area. In the valleys beneath the mountain, life goes on, rich and good.

Tonight, Warren decided, I'll call Mom and tell her I have a new friend who lives in Gram's neighborhood. Mom would be glad about that.

CHAPTER

14

"Good news," Betsy said as she and Warren walked into class together. "Creampuff got adopted last night."

In the month since they escaped from the volcano, Warren had helped Betsy exercise Creampuff every day. The little dog had lost a pound, but she was still much too heavy.

"The man who took her is on a diet himself," Betsy said. "Creampuff's problem didn't bother him one bit. He said he needs a diet buddy to walk with."

"I'll miss Creampuff," Warren said.

"So will I," Betsy said. "I cried when she left. But I called the Purebred Dog Rescue right away and told them I'm ready for another foster dog."

Mr. Munson tapped his desk with a ruler, signaling the students to be quiet.

"I finished grading your reports last night," Mr. Munson said, "and I am pleased with your work."

Sighs of relief whispered through the room.

"One report was particularly well written," Mr. Munson went on. "It is twenty-seven pages long and lists more than a dozen sources. I want to congratulate Warren and Betsy for getting the first A-plus I have ever given in this class."

Warren and Betsy grinned at each other.

Skipper poked Warren. When Warren looked, Skipper raised his right eyebrow up and down while he wiggled his left ear.

Mr. Munson said, "The idea of writing the report as a diary, as if they had actually been there, was original and effective. As I read, I almost believed that Betsy and Warren had lived through the eruption of Mount Saint Helens themselves, although I know that isn't possible."

"Of course not," Warren said.

Betsy's eyes twinkled at him, but she said nothing.

"It's clear," Mr. Munson said, "that Betsy and Warren did extensive research on their topic."

That's for sure, Warren thought. He had never before worked so hard on an assignment, or been so interested in what he learned.

Warren had read the newspapers from 1980 that were on microfiche at the Issaquah Library. In one of them he found a list of survivors who were rescued by helicopter, and saw the name *Rhonda Huron.* Was she the woman in the red car? Her husband had called her Rhonda, but Warren didn't know the last name. He wondered how she could have escaped if her husband and child didn't. The list identified one man as a logger; Warren wondered if it was one of the men he had warned.

When he read in a library book that the lightning during the eruption was caused by static electricity, and that it was multicolored because of the volcanic gases in the air, he couldn't wait to tell Betsy.

Betsy learned that the ash did not hurt the earth where it fell. "But some victims died from inhaling the ash," she told Warren. "During the eruption, the superheated ash seriously burned their lungs."

Warren remembered how hard it had been to catch his breath, and how hot the ash had felt on his lips.

"Inhaling small amounts of ash, as we did," Betsy went on, "was not harmful."

"We were lucky," Warren said, and they gave each other relieved high fives.

One Saturday Betsy's family took Warren with them to the Mount Saint Helens Visitor Center. The road leading to the Visitor Center offered stunning views of the volcano; Warren and Betsy had stared at the huge crater, remembering their close call with disaster.

At the Visitor Center they watched a movie and read every word of the various displays.

"Did you know," Betsy said as she read one display, "that five hundred forty million tons of ash were emitted during the eruption, and that in two weeks some of that ash had circled the earth?"

"It was a mistake to bring her here," Lori said. "She'll be quoting weird statistics for months."

The Volcano Disaster

By the time Warren and Betsy finished writing their report, they were experts on the topic of Mount Saint Helens.

Mr. Munson began handing back the graded papers. "Attached to each report," he said, "is your assignment for the next report."

Everyone groaned.

"Don't we get to rest in between projects?" Skipper said.

"You've rested for a week while I read and graded these," Mr. Munson said. "Since these first reports were so good, I've decided to keep the same partners for the second report."

Warren smiled at Betsy. She smiled back.

Warren remembered how annoyed he had felt when Betsy was assigned to be his partner the first time. He had felt awkward with her, and didn't know what to say. Now he was eager to do another report with her.

Warren thought, I didn't want to work with her because I didn't really know her. But when you survive a volcano with someone, and share a secret like the Instant Commuter, you get to know that person in

131

a hurry. And it doesn't matter if your friend is a girl or a boy.

Betsy still startled him when she blurted odd facts, but her information was usually interesting, and her memory had been useful when they wrote about the eruption.

They still had not told anyone about the Instant Commuter. They were cleaning it and trying to improve the design to eliminate the wind.

Mr. Munson handed the report to Betsy. She carried it to the worktable where Warren was, and sat beside him. They admired the big red A-plus on the top page.

The new assignment was paper-clipped to the front of the report. They read it together.

The Armistice Day Blizzard
November 11, 1940
Minnesota, Wisconsin, and other
northern states.

"Wear your long underwear," Betsy whispered. "It will be cold when we get there."

"I am not going to Minnesota during a blizzard," Warren said. "A blizzard means tons of snow and freezing temperatures."

Betsy pointed to the A-plus. "Did you ever get one of those before?"

"Are you kidding? No way."

"Neither have I. My parents will go into orbit with glee. Maybe I'll ask for a raise in my allowance."

"My mom will be thrilled, too," Warren said. "So will Gram."

"Next time we'll be more careful with the Instant Commuter," Betsy said. "We'll stay together, and we'll know exactly what to do to get home safely."

"We might have gotten the A-plus without the trip we took. We did a lot of research."

"That's true," Betsy said. "But the reason we wanted to do so much research was because we had actually experienced the eruption. Would we really have written twenty-seven pages if we didn't have a personal interest in the subject? I don't think so."

"You are crazy," Warren said. "We nearly got cremated by a volcano, and now you want to get buried by a blizzard."

"I have no intention of being buried," Betsy said. "But I do plan to get another A-plus."

Warren thought about it. They did know more about the Instant Commuter now, and they could control their destination. "We would have to plan exactly when to go," he said, "and how and when to come home."

"Of course."

"I get cold just thinking about all that snow."

"Even though all snow crystals are six-sided," Betsy said, "no two are ever exactly the same pattern. They're like fingerprints. Jillions and jillions of snow crystals, and each one is different."

"I wonder how many jillion fell to the ground on November eleventh, 1940," Warren said.

"Don't forget your boots," said Betsy.

To learn more about Mount Saint Helens and other volcanoes:

Disastrous Volcanoes
Melvin Berger
Franklin Watts (New York, NY, 1981)

Earth Afire!
R.V. Fodor
William Morrow & Co. (New York, NY, 1981)

How Did We Find Out About Volcanoes?
Isaac Asimov
Walker and Co. (New York, NY, 1981)

Mt. St. Helens: *A Sleeping Volcano Awakes*
Marian T. Place
Dodd, Mead (New York, NY, 1981)

Volcano
Brian Knapp
Steck-Vaughn Co. (Austin, TX, 1990)

Volcanoes
Jacqueline Dineen
Gloucester Press (New York, NY, 1991)

Peg Kehret

Volcanoes: *Earth's Inner Fire*
Sally M. Walker
Carolrhoda Books, Inc. (Minneapolis, MN, 1994)

Why Mount St. Helens Blew Its Top
Kathryn A. Goldner and Carole G. Vogel
Dillion Press, Inc. (Minneapolis, MN, 1981)

DISCARD